# Everything in
# Its Right Place

# Everything in Its Right Place

Olivia Parker

Print information available on the last page.

Rev. date: 08/27/2019

**To order additional copies of this book, contact:**
Xlibris
0-800-443-678
www.Xlibris.co.nz
Orders@Xlibris.co.nz
801728

# EVERYTHING IN ITS RIGHT PLACE
By Olivia Parker

I was a mystery to myself
I couldn't even recognise my own face
I was a stranger to love
Since she vanished without a trace
Life as I knew it was out of control
I strayed out of time and space while I waited
For everything to be in its right place

I felt like I was looking in on my life
I didn't understand the purpose of roses and white lace
I wasn't schooled to appreciate honesty
Life was just another challenge – another race
I was in the game simply for the chase nothing was gained
Yet everything was in its right place

It was touch and go; everyone to his own
For a while I saw life as a game of charades
I'd won some, lost some, gave love away
So I handed back her heart, unable to keep up with the pace
She left no note, and took no suitcase
Too late I've realised she gave me what time cannot erase –
Her love has put
Everything in its right place

## 2003 – 2010 (Reworked 2018)

For my cousin Gareth - Here's to that message in that empty white wine bottle in the winter of 2003. Thank you for the support through the tears, the laughter and the *"I-told-you-so's"*. Here's to the hero that you are, and the kind of man every woman should get to know in her lifetime and appreciate.

For Lynette, Esther, Georgia and Imelda – thank you for being my soundboard during one of the toughest times in my life.

For my colleagues from the WCPP for the services they provide to the people of the Western Cape Province.

Also, to my cousin Orrin and your colleagues - the men and women of the South African Police Service who sacrifice their time, family lives, and their own well being by striving to create the safe, crime-free country of opportunity that Nelson Mandela had dreamed it to be.

# PROLOGUE

## Cape Town, Youth Day, 16 June 2008
## 20:45PM

The inadequate lamp washed the small sitter in a channeling amber setting.

He had been reduced to nothing.

He had forgotten what it was like to make his top of the range double bed. Clothes that were way overdue for the Laundromat lay strewn across the floor.

Empty whiskey bottles replaced what once used to be known to him as dishes. It too lay scattered.

His black hair was a thick greasy mess. A once handsome, well-groomed face was grazed with stubble. The deep crease between his brows seemed to be the only proof that his brain was still in operation.

Smoke from a cigar reached his nostrils. He could see it from the corner of his eye. It was still in the abalone shell where he had left it. A cup of black coffee stood beside it. A white filmy substance had gathered on the top since he had left it there all of three days ago.

Dressed in a white shirt and black three-piece suit, now rumpled, was the only reminder of the luxury he had once been used to. Now, his bare feet were shoved into exquisite leather shoes. His jacket was undone, as too were the top three buttons of his shirt.

The plain black tie lay beside him on the arm of the worn single seater couch he was slouched in. His legs were slightly parted as he rested his forearms on his thighs.

His head dropped. With a half-drunk bottle of whiskey dangling from the fingertips of his left hand and a .22 caliber revolver firm in the other, he shot back in the chair.

The walls seemed to be closing in on him.

Torturing screams were coming from the walls.

He was convinced that it wasn't in his head. He heard the familiar sound of *her* voice.

It was real, he thought.

He wasn't crazy.

Not him!

He started pacing the confines of the cage he felt he was in. He needed to escape somehow. He needed the release of *her* tormenting last scream that seemed to have gone on and on long after it should have been silenced by her devastating fate. Increasing echoes now came from the walls.

It wasn't just *hers* anymore.

Now, screams from his mother and father tortured him.

It seemed to be increasing and now belonged to faceless people that were the cause of him being where he was right now. Insane.

And right now, he was going to make them pay.

The voices sounded muffled to his ears now.

The only thing he could hear was the pounding of his heart over his shallow breathing.

The cigar was now just a mini rod of ash in the empty shell.

Shaking his head frantically and raising fists to his ears, he shot out of his chair with a choked frustrated scream.

He paced the little flat, feeling like a caged animal. Rage built up inside him like heated lava ready to erupt.

The music blaring from the stereo seemed to be brainwashing him – motivating his malicious thoughts of revenge.

How could *she* hurt him that way?

How could *she* lie to him?

Why would the forces of nature allow him to love *her* and then take *her* away from *him*, why *him*?

The universe was going to pay somehow – a universe that dealt him nothing but a bad hand of solitaire. He could no longer command the hand he had been dealt. With bloodshot eyes he exploded through the haphazard door and stumbled into the wet cold night.

Traffic lights up yonder and lilac street lamps were mirrored on the wet tar that stretched from the front of the alley into all directions. He gave a mocking laugh. He used to see life as a road map and now he literally had to choose a path – not one to live, but one to die.

Puffs of cold vapor escaped from his mouth. His thighs slouched slowly as he walked, draining the last of the whiskey. He wiped his mouth with the sleeve of his jacket and flung the bottle aside. It had hit something but he didn't care until debris stirred behind him and a homeless man dressed in tattered camouflage jumped out and called after him. "Asshole! What the hell do you think this is a litter box, pussy?"

He turned to face the man whose teeth were rotting out of his head. Had he not bought that same homeless man a takeaway three days ago? He couldn't remember. He turned slowly and raised the gun. The moonlight glinted off the steel of the barrel and he opened fire. He didn't stay to check if the man had been struck, but more homeless people crawled out of holes and makeshift shelters to see the commotion.

"Hey! Come back here! You've just killed a man," shouted a woman dressed in badly soiled clothes and a dirty red bandana.

He turned to face her and raised his gun one more time.

It had started to drizzle.

He squeezed the trigger and watched as her body slumped to the ground.

Sirens where closing in a few blocks away. He could see the red and blue lights reflecting from gaps in the side roads, he didn't care.

He turned the corner and found himself in a crowded main road where young executives were enjoying pizza and beer.

The sidewalk was streaming with giggling women competing for the attention of well-dressed men in business suits and carrying briefcases.

"Hi," said a model-faced blonde as he eyed her with disaffection. She was clearly a high profile prostitute from an exclusive escort agency. "Looks like you could do with a bath and a brush big spender." The girls in her clique, dressed equally scantily, giggled as they surrounded her and quieted down almost instantly when the barrel of his gun settled between their friend's eyes.

Blood sprayed onto the panic-stricken girls as they scurried away screaming. The sidewalk cleared up and waiters dived behind tables as the gunman started opening fire. It had begun to rain a little harder. His hair was flattened against his forehead. He raised his face to the sky and found himself in the middle of the road.

A dozen of police vehicles surrounded him, doors were swinging wide open to served as bullet shields.

He could feel his teeth were bare. That usually meant that he was smiling. He caught a glimpse of himself in a restaurant window. His teeth were bare, yes. But he wasn't smiling. He looked scary with his eyes bugged out the way they were. He laughed – snorted - as he made contact with a man dressed in a gray overcoat and a thick mustache. He raised his gun and aimed for the left breast pocket of his coat when a biting pain in his right arm caused his gun to drop to the wet road.

A shower of bullets hailed on him. Each one entered his body with exploding numbness. The last bullet entered his chest.

He looked down astonished at the blood spraying out of him like he had been a human fountain. It soon became a streamlet and he dropped to his knees.

Blue and red lights were becoming blurry.

Blood gushed out of his body and joined the little stream the rain had formed along the pavement where it disappeared into a storm water drain.

The world seemed to darken around the edges. He had the salty taste of blood in his mouth and he gurgled. The rain was pouring into his bullet wounds washing him clean from the stains life had inflicted on his soul and carried him into a dark echoing tunnel that had no end and least of all, it was free from the sound of *her* voice…

# CHAPTER ONE

*Hout Street, Cape Town*
*Friday, 14 March 2008*
**16:45PM**

The lights had flickered on and everywhere around him the sound of rebooted computers drowned the silence. It was the third time this week that the power had gone off for no particular reason and the generators hadn't even kicked in. Wesley Johnson looked up from his desk at the man who had emerged through the metal doors of the elevator.

"I have it under control," said the man lugging a blue toolbox. He was wearing gray overalls and badly worn sneakers.

Wesley's lips curled in appreciation. He remembered only too well how hard his father had worked. Years in construction had made provision for his son to attend the best schools to receive a good education. Now that Wesley had the perfect job he could support both his parents. Although he lived in a sought-after flat in Cape Town CBD, he visited his folks whenever he could. Being an only child meant his parents was lonely without him back in Strandfontein. With his father recovering from a stroke and his mother's high blood pressure, Wesley saw them more often than he did in the past. He had arranged for them to spend the nearing Easter weekend at Sun City. They deserved a break from the violence of the Cape Flats, especially with the ever growing informal settlements that seemed to be getting closer to the tail end of Mitchell's Plain where safety was still reasonably okay. He sat back before logging himself back onto the server. With the takeover of one of the local banks by an international European financial giant, he would be working right through the Easter break.

The light in the far corner of the open plan office fluttered on. Wesley rose slightly from his chair to find the permanent moping Jacques Cloete stretching and yawning as he shuffled about.

"Can you believe we have to work while the rest of the guys are at the Waterfront *suiping*?" Jacques's slurry speech often had the staff laughing. He was a typical *boerseun* with thick blonde hair, dressed like a surfer – complete with board shorts and flip-flops if not gracing the office barefoot. Heavy lids always hid his pale blue eyes. He slumped in his chair and turned on the television overhead. "Hey *broer*," he bobbed his head at Wesley. "The new media place in Greenpoint invited us to the launch of their new account thanks to your quick thinking with getting their system operational. It's today. Spread the word okay? I'll forget once I start reprogramming this damn network."

Wesley looked at his colleague quizzically. "Reprogramming? No one mentioned anything to me about it."

Jacque drank deeply from a bottle of cola, "Ja *boet*. It will take me at least five hours. Then I can sleep off the banana *blaartjies*."

Wesley decided to end the conversation. He had been warned that despite being a whiz, Jacques had some scaly reputation and scary acquaintances. He has been rumoured to run up tabs at notorious informal taverns on the Cape Flats. Jacques was also constantly borrowing money from the staff, paying it back, and then borrowing it again. Wesley knew from his time at university that fruit tobacco was used mainly to disguise the smell of *dagga*.

The new European account meant that Wesley was now directly talking to the Director of Operations at the international IT support firm, instead of going through channels. It was a good feeling knowing that he was trusted with this much responsibility. The phone rang and he quickly slipped the headset on and adjusted the mouthpiece. "Helpdesk," he said.

Wesley was used to the accents of foreigners by now. Apart from a mainstream Swedish bank, his other account was with an American air charter company. Bookings and other technical services were provided to the airline.

*"Mango-Orange-Nectarine-Tango-Elephant-Litchi-Litchi-Orange. First name: Litchi-Una-Tango-Zebra-Indigo-Orange,"* came the impatient voice on the other end of the line. *"I'm going to use my buddy pass for my employee Tango-Hippo-Orange-Mango-Apple-Strawberry. First name: Apple-Nectarine-Nectarine-Elephant. You got that?"*

"Copy that Mr Montello," Wesley sat frantically typing on the keyboard. "Your flight leaves JFK International at 09h00, New York time on Friday." Wesley read off the other necessary details and finally said, "I will email the flight details to your office, sir. Are the contact details still the same? Email address, and landlines, faxes and physical and postal addresses?" Wesley listened for a while. He checked the visual of the call. "Son of a bitch!" he stared at the screen in disbelief. "He hung up on me." Wesley checked the time on his workstation. It was time to hit the road and meet his good friends Daryl Cozyn and Alan Davids for a drink. He checked the email from Jacques with the details of the ConNet Media function, and called the boys. He would opt for time with his good old varsity buddies than the office crowed at the Victoria and Alfred Waterfront any day.

## The Krimson Kimono, Greenpoint, Cape Town
## Friday, 14 March 2008
## 19:21PM

The stuffy kitchen was the first thing that needed attention after she finished her exam, noted Kristen Katts. She had bought this establishment with part of her savings that had been transferred into a local bank account. By the time she got back from the Baxter Theatre, there was already a growing queue to enter the Krimson Kimono, as she'd named the coffee shop come sports bar. The Krimson Kimono had a very intimate neo jazz pub on its first floor that proved to be a great attraction to young and upcoming executives.

She had changed into her black uniform shirt so quickly, she hadn't even realised that she had missed a button. She turned to the opening swinging-door that led to the bar counter. The manager she'd hired when she'd started out, Natasha Meyer stood propped against the wall. "Cash bar, ladies," she called. "I'm sending in my four waitresses. All orders are to be placed at the bar and paid for. We're not going to survive if we have the waitresses going around. The waitresses will just deliver to the tables. And, good news," she smiled at Kristen, but spoke to the kitchen staff. "The boss requested that we only do hot chips today – medium and large only. The extra sauce didn't arrive yet, so we're going to have to use sachets from the store," she motioned to a doorless room beside the stainless steel freezers. "We did receive a shitload of fries, which you will find in those freezers along that wall." Natasha walked as she spoke and pointed out. "We also have an overflow of ciders, beers, spirits and soft drinks. Use ice from the white chest freezer only. We may have a problem for tomorrow night's lineup if we use the fresh ice we made yesterday."

Natasha glanced at Kristen one last time with a teasing grin. "The boss could walk in at any moment and no one would know, so please, keep up the smiles." She glanced at the students dressed in short red kimonos. Their faces were made to look like those of geishas. White ankle socks and Chinese pumps, black wigs and chopsticks rounded off the look as they sighed in unison. "That guy at table five with the red hair and freckles tried to flirt with me," shuddered the shortest waitress, known as Ling. In their disguises, no one knew what they actually looked like except Natasha. Their nameplates were all false as well. They answered to Yoko, Ling, Mia and Ty.

Kristen laughed. "Why are you wincing?" she asked with her thick British public school accent.

Ling rolled her eyes animatedly that made the entire kitchen staff laugh. "Take a peek," she motioned in the general direction of table five.

Natasha got the laughing women under control with a sharp "*yo*". "Do I need to remind you that we have executives of a media company and Torea performing live tonight, so please earn your overtime and for my students, earn your tuition tonight." With that she turned abruptly and left. The women fell into an immediate chatter as Kristen started tearing plastic from ciders and stacking them in the available fridges.

It was a relief that none of them knew she was the boss, or that she was the daughter of a feared Mafia boss.

For safety purposes, Kristina Katherine Montello had fled to South Africa to pursue a career in theatre. She had to leave London as the British government refused her citizenship or even refugee status. South Africa was a completely different case. It was too easy to blend in and even easier to obtain refugee status. No extensive background checks meant she was safe from being refused citizenship – live in hope that her father never sets foot on the West Coast and decide to start a *franchise* in the already drug-infested Mother City.

She turned at the sound of Natasha rushing through the doors. "Table five needs a basket of hot chips – on the house. They've just ordered ten beers. Kristen, will you take it out? Charlie's Angels are battling with the drunken sales reps from the media company."

Kristen laughed, "Of course." She took the basket and pushed her way through the queue at the bar to the infamous table five. Three young men about her age sat laughing over frothy beer and cheered glassy eyed at the singer on the stage. She had forked out a good few thousand rand for the talented entertainment. It was a good thing that people were actually enjoying the seventeen year old, *Torea*.

Kristen slid half across the table to retrieve four empty beer bottles before placing the basket of fries on the table. The smell of warm vinegar made her wince. She shook unruly curls from her face as she gently ran a disinfectant cloth over the table. The second she'd lifted the cloth from the table her gaze locked with dark eyes. He was looking at her suggestively, holding her gaze and daring her to look away.

"The next round is on you, Wesley," a husky voice sounded from behind her. Kristen looked at the red-haired man. Despite herself, she smiled as she remembered the waitress's words earlier in the kitchen. He was very pale in complexion with bright orange hair and freckles. His brown eyes were locked on the man who had so intensely watched her. Suddenly nervous, Kristen risked one more look at Wesley before she backed away from the table enough to turn tail and head back to the kitchen. He was tall and lean, yet his forearms were muscular. His careless dark hair was slightly too long for a man, but it somehow suited him. There was an air about him that made him seem fashionably sensitive, but unconcerned at the same time.

Before she went into the kitchen, she stole one last glance at him. He was still seated, but it seemed as though he was the object of Torea's interest as well. The singer was practically flashing him her boobs.

A disgusted sound escaped Kristen. In her opinion, Capetonian women just kept proving to be loose.

Although the swivel-head fans were turned on full power, it did nothing to minimise the thick accumulating smoke that settled over a greater part of the pub.

The dark local beauty and over rated singer was dressed in purple and silver sequence and feathers that looked about as suitable for the can-can than for a seventeen year old pop icon. A spiky, brilliant scarlet wig with purple streaks graced the top of Torea's head. Heavy silver earrings and matching chunky silver accessories clanked over her delicate arms. An assortment of eight dainty charm bracelets dangled around either ankle where silver gladiator stilettos met the jingling misfits.

Wesley strained uncomfortably against the backrest of his chair. Torea had chosen him as part of her props for the delivering of her final song for the evening. It was a raunchy cover version of Paula Cole's *Feelin' Love*. Torea had gone the complete route of dancing on the table top and shimmying all the way down in a maneuver that saw her sharp behind hit the table top in a circular motion before she rose and saddled Wesley in a skillfully practiced manner.

Women were holding drinks and clutch bags above their heads as they cheered while Torea was slowly sliding off the black blazer from Wesley's powerful set shoulders. The way she rubbed up against his lap left her intimate part burning and throbbing through his pants. He felt her grow hot and wet and instead of becoming turned on, he was uncomfortable and disgusted.

She was singing the second verse of the song when she grabbed his tie and arched her back far enough so that her back was pressed flat against his lap. Still laying face up, she made a sexual gesture lifting her behind slightly before pulling herself back up by his tie.

Around them, the crowd had grown more thrilled and ecstatic. Men were shouting in awe and women seemed to be physically stimulated by the tone and the lyrics of the song. Torea glided off his lap and swiveled her lithe little body so that she was still sitting on his lap with her back towards his chest.

With the microphone steady around her ear, she used her free hands to seek out his hands blindly as she guided them from her knees to her breasts in a slow deliberate method that had people shrieking with excitement. She bounced up and down on Wesley's lap in perfect timing with the rhythm of the song before she fell back against him at the exact moment the song came to an end.

Kristen watched from the stairs. She could see the back of Wesley's head now. Torea was settled in a sidesaddle fashion on his lap. She was whispering in his ear while the crowd had drowned the place in applause and then breaking out with a steady "we want more".

Reluctantly, she waded back to the platform that served as a stage. "Let's hear it for Mr Wesley Johnson, ladies and gents." Torea motioned to Wesley with a shaky hand. "One last song then I really have to be on my way," she announced. "Just because you're such a great crowd…" A quick word to the bandleader and she was singing yet another ballad from her new album. It was a song that had a dreamy feel to it, but the rush of people down the stairs made Kristen return to the kitchen. She entered as Natasha plopped onto an empty beer crate. "That girl is good! Quite a little entertainer, that one," she bobbed her head.

Kristen smiled at her and back into the flushed faces of the kitchen staff. "I'm glad the boss made such a good choice."

"Are you kidding me?" Natasha roared. "It was a brilliant choice. Did you see the sweat running down that poor man's face when she rubbed up against him? I swear he would've *ejaculated* if she didn't stop!"

Kristen giggled along with the staff, but it was a phony burst of laughter on her behalf. Why did it bother her that Torea was flirting with a stranger whom she'd never laid eyes on except tonight? Was it because there was some sort of chemical reaction when their gazes met for a few moments? Could it be that his dark gaze had stirred up an emotion inside her that she so longed for that it was making her jealous. Jealous? That was preposterous! No, there just wasn't enough oxygen in the Krimson Kimono. She smoothed her hands over the front of her shirt and took a deep breath. She needed a smoke and a *Vodka Collins*. "Natasha, could I bum a smoke?" she didn't wait for an answer. She dug her hand into the older woman's black apron and took out a long slim cigarette, before walking to the door.

"Kristen!" Natasha's voice had her whipping around. "You going to light it with your finger?" she threw a black lighter at Kristen.

Kristen smiled her thanks and made her way out of the pub.

# CHAPTER TWO

*The Krimson Kimono, Greenpoint*
*Tuesday, 18 March 2008*
**12:00PM**

The high noon sun scourged the tar as beach-goers started streaming into the overnight popular *Krimson Kimono*. The beach pub come coffee shop had many owners trading the intimate establishment under various different names before now. It was unusually hot for late March – the end of the tourist season that usually left the Western Cape in a slight economic recession every year. But this year seemed to be different. Foreigners were viewing flats and other sources of accommodation for the approaching soccer world cup.

Wesley had dealt with a huge chunk of those foreigners. The frequent blackouts weren't a very commendable role player in it that it took a good ten minutes for the backup generators to kick in on the work front. It was a mess! It meant that extra cost was involved on the company's expense to reconnect with clients and apart from the delay; it could possibly mean that certain data in the system was vulnerable during those strained moments of total disconnection.

Wesley peeked over the top of his electronic notebook as the spunky redhead manageress stepped into view. He'd heard one of the bar hands call her Natasha last Friday. Since the Krimson Kimono didn't trade on a Monday, it was an excruciating wait over the weekend for him. It wasn't the happy hour beer special; the free basket of hot chips with every ten beers purchased; the sexy radio sales reps from ConNet Media in their black pinstripe suits; or even the scented business card he had been slipped by the local singing sensation Torea, who performed four singles in promotion of her new album – or in promotion of getting him in the sack, he thought with a shrug. It was the curvy, tanned waitress he'd seen that night. She was the reason he woke up every hour thinking of the many ways that he could make love to her. The way her soft honey-brown curls fell into the heart-shaped persistently was the closest thing to magical he'd experienced. Even the absent minded way she shook the curls from her big dark green eyes made the harsh overhead light dance over her striking features. She smelt of oven grease, beer and oddly expensive perfume for a kitchen hand. Her black shirt was missing a button and was innocently exposing a very sexy black and pink lacy bra. Heavily chested, voluptuous women were not his usual categorical packages of interest, but for some peculiar reason it made her look like a goddess and completely lured him to an unexpected impassioned obsession. Just the thought of her sent his blood rushing to his genitalia. There was something about the way she held his gaze that made him go back today. He waited. There was no sign of her the entire morning or even now. His off day was turning out to be a very disappointing one when a sudden thump on the table beside him jerked Wesley back to reality.

Natasha stood towering over him, fists on her hips, "Your avocado and feta tramezzini."

"Thank you." Wesley hesitated for a moment before he spoke. "The girl that works here," he started nervously. "She worked Friday. She didn't wear the Chinese garb dressy like the others. She had on a black shirt."

Natasha pursed her lips as she patted the pockets of the apron.

"Curls and green eyes," Wesley offered.

"What about her?" Natasha asked lighting a long slim cigarette. "Got a complaint?" she exhaled a generous cloud of smoke.

Wesley shook his head. "No. I'm just curious. I've never seen her here before. She just sort of stood out."

Natasha fixed him with a quizzical look, "She helps out when the boss can *afford* to have her here."

The way she said the word "afford" had Wesley shifting with impatience. "I'm talking about the waitress," he said.

"Yes," Natasha said taking a long drag before exhaling slowly. "I know who you are referring to."

Wesley snapped his laptop shut and slumped back in his chair. He watched as Natasha's eyes narrowed knowingly. "Its best you let her be, boyo," she said. She took one last steady drag from her long white satin tip before stubbing it out in the unused ashtray on Wesley's table. "She isn't looking for any romantic attachments."

The fork felt heavy in his hand as he poked at the delicately trimmed orange slice and carrot garnish on the side of the black square-shaped plate. "She was just so exquisite," he said almost to himself.

Natasha slumped one of her shoulders and tapped an indecisive hand on the backrest of the chair closest to her. She let out a heavy sigh. "You know that new revue restaurant in Observatory? The one named after some fruit," her brows drew together in a deep thoughtful plough. "I can never remember the name," she sighed.

Wesley moved the soft bread to the side of his mouth with his tongue. "Hmmm!" he motioned in recognition. "The Stuffed Pineapple?"

Natasha slapped her thigh. "That's the one."

"What about it?"

"She'll be there tonight. Although I must warn you to please *not* do anything stupid."

A smile spread across his face despite himself. "I just want to talk to her." Before he could get any more information out of her, Natasha was swiftly moving toward a hand waving her to an outside sidewalk table. Wesley checked the time on his wristwatch. There was still plenty of time to hit the gym and shower before he would see the woman who had so easily haunted his dreams. He would check the internet for the details of the *Stuffed Pineapple* and reserve a table. He thought of calling Daryl to join him, but decided against it. If he was going to at least get her to join him for coffee, it was only going to be *her* with him. Besides,

Dylan was acting really peculiar lately with hardly any time to spare for his friends.

### The Stuffed Pineapple Restaurant and Revue Bar, Observatory, Cape Town
### Tuesday, 18 March 2008
### 20:50pm

It was a habit.

One that he'd been teased about over the years, but Wesley was a man who was obsessed with neatness. He spent a lot of time on grooming and keeping his bachelor flat in tiptop shape. It was something that his mother had instilled in him as a little boy. Even in the darkness of the restaurant, Wesley lined up the array of sauces that was placed in a mini replica of a wooden crate that was placed in the centre of his table.

The Stuffed Pineapple was hosting a national tour of a *proudly gay* music act. The food was good old fashion green bean stew. Although he had to admit that his mother's cooking was ten times better, Wesley let out a satisfied sigh. He glanced around the long narrow establishment. Small square tables were pushed together to accommodate parties exceeding four people. Black and yellow tablecloths were neatly coordinated with a fresh pineapple in the centre of every table, which sprouted a strategic white candle in the middle of the green spikes.

He'd been here a good hour, and there was no sign of the object of his fascination. Just as his second whiskey and tonic was brought to the table. The lights went out.

"Damnit," came the startled voice of the young waitress. Around him, the friction of lighters gave into little tongues of amber light. He watched with growing amusement as the clumsy blonde lit the candle on his table. Her voice was soft and childlike when she spoke. "The kitchen is now closed, sir. The bar will be re-opened during the interval which is roughly forty minutes from now." She quickly stacked the used crockery onto each other and reached for the empty glass with her free hand. "Enjoy the show."

"Thank you," he said as a mechanical sound beamed from the stage.

*"Jacks and Jills… please welcome on stage the one – the only – the gorgeous – the beautiful – the extraordinary – the talented - the very tall – very confused -"* the male voice was drowned by a sudden burst of laughter from the audience - *"…and the very dramatic Mincing Monique!"* More applause from the audience before a very elaborately sequenced hat came into view. As the light slowly fixated and expanded over the giant of a drag queen, the spectacular costume of lilacs, yellows and greens came into full view. A second later music from the 1950's and 1960's erupted into a very entertaining storyline and brought a close to the funniest, cleverly dramatised live performance he'd seen to date. The gnawing inside him was once again a raw primal feel when he couldn't spot her anywhere. His eyes kept returning to the trio at the far end of a corner bar separate from the main bar. They were dressed in matching black and white suits to the likes of Charlie Chapman – complete with hats and mustaches. There was something naturally feminine about the way they sipped the strawberry daiquiris that was set down in front of them. Wesley was wrenched back to reality when the sudden queue from a piano and a bright spotlight graced the stage. Mincing Monique stood on the stage dressed like a vintage gentleman, microphone in hand. He fell into song with the Frank Senatra classic *What Makes a Man.*

It won a standing ovation. He bowed gracefully and waved into the crowd to familiar faces.

It took Wesley a moment before he realised the "Benny" the crowd was chanting was Mincing Monique's actual name.

"Thank you! Now give yourselves a round of applause," Benny encouraged. "That's the way to go!" He took a deep breath. "Ladies and Gentlemen, may I introduce my brilliant co-actors?" he motioned to the side of the stage where five other drag queens all now in formal men's clothing gracefully glided to his side. He ranted off their names in a quick liquid manner. His hand shifted in the direction of the corner bar. "And last but not least, my stagehands: Dianne Jeppe, Kristen Katts and Freda Goosen!"

Wesley's head snapped back to the trio who were now making their way up to the stage. They stood on Benny's left, on the opposite side of the men who part took in the act. They fell into a quick, but hilarious tap routine that had the crowd in an appreciative laugh. In a fluid motion, with their backs turned to the audience, they removed their hats while doing a backward gallop. Their hair was in an identical knot at the nape of their necks. In a heart stopping second, they turned. The spotlight froze on them as they paused – facing straight ahead with their hats in the hands of their extended right arms. More applause.

Wesley's mouth fell open and the bottom of his stomach dropped out. It was *her*. She was the stagehand in the middle. Her name was Kristen Katts. She looked outwardly jovial as she made her way back to her strawberry daiquiri. Giggles turned to light chatter and eventually turned into an undecipherable hum. It was now or never. This was the moment he'd been waiting for all of four days, and now, standing twenty feet away from her, he wasn't too sure that he could do it - at least not while his stomach was in his throat.

She had had fun tonight, Kristen thought as she listened to the other two girls chatted over her. They were the same height, similar in built and the last similarity – they were all brunettes.

Dianna was the soft-spoken and all-round sweetheart. She was a very talented playwright, engaged to a lawyer. She was talking about the uncomfortable way her panties were creeping into her behind. "Christ! It doesn't help that these chairs are unforgivably high."

Freda eyed her with glistening beady eyes just preying on a line to turn into a witty, but fanatically funny joke. She was a natural. "Lucky panties," she drawled in her southern suburb private school accent. "You are lucky to have a lucky packet ring on that bony finger of yours. You're not the one who'll be mistaken for a gay man with that bone structure of yours." She glimpsed over her shoulder and spotted a rather confused looking man stroll over to them with a drink in one hand and the other impassively shoved into the pocket of his charcoal suit. She swiveled back around in her chair. "That is exactly what I mean," she rolled her eyes heavenward. "A perfectly handsome specimen makes his way over here thinking we're all gay men!"

Dianna giggled as she lifted the black straw out of her drink. She watched merrily as Freda animatedly yanked the artificial yellow and red hibiscus from Kristen's drink and stuck it in her hair, securing it with the pin holding down her outgrown fringe. The movement left the disturbed curl swinging gently into her bewildered face. "Close your mouth honey," Freda smiled lazily at Kristen. He is gay after all." She stole a last look over her shoulder. "What a waste."

"Which one?" Dianne leaned forward to lock gazes with Freda.

"Four 'o clock." She winked.

Dianna looked confused. "Your four o' clock or my four o' clock?" just then her eyes widened and she gasped, "Oh Kris! He is coming toward you!" she squealed in excitement.

Freda leaned forward and engaged Dianna with wide-eyed horror. "Don't call her Kris! He might think she's a transvestite!"

Kristen tensed as she felt the masculine presence. It didn't take long to smell the well-balanced cologne that flowed from his skin. She was almost afraid to turn around, even when she heard her two friends clearing their throats so deliberately - it was almost embarrassing. Winning the attention of the opposite sex wasn't something she was used to or needed right now. She was gathering her thoughts and her composure when she felt the slow pivoting motion of her chair. Her eyes were focused on the neatly manicured hands that barely brushed the side of her thighs. Her eyes slowly trailed up the white shirt to the undone buttons where a tie should have been clipped. His lean masculine jaw. His clean-shaven cheeks and his slightly parted full mouth. Although she was sitting on the high stool, her eyes were level with his mouth. She took in a deep steady breath before tilting her head back. She felt the blood rush to her face as colour flared over her cheeks. "It's you…" she blinked in disbelief.

"You're Kristen?" He asked.

She nodded, unable to speak.

"I'd like to buy you a drink," he smiled.

He was handsome. The easy smile that played over his mouth was sending her pulse into overdrive.

"A drink?" her voice sounded strangled.

She heard Freda mumble something that sounded like "u-oh… she's in trouble…"

Dianna cleared her throat sensing that Kristen needed some motivation. She risked a look at Freda who was miming, "A paper bag. Get her a brown paper bag. She needs to hyperventilate," her fist flew to her mouth in demonstration.

Dianna smiled at the visibly uncertain man in front of Kristen. "Hi, I'm Dianna and that-" she motioned to Freda "- is Freda. So how do you know Kristen…um…?"

"Wesley. My name is Wesley." He answered without shifting his gaze from Kristen. "I don't know Kristen. I've only seen her once before."

Freda cleared her throat and pivoted her own chair to stare at Wesley. "Yet, here you are. What a coincidence?"

Dianna nudged Kristen playfully. "Didn't you say you wanted to try the piña colada?"

Kristen nodded. "Yes. I'd like one of those."

"Kristen," Dianna leaned toward her slightly so that Wesley could hear. "Why don't you go with Wesley to the bar? You know how Lucas gets when he sees a new face. He might think Wesley is – " she visibly fished for a word.

"– gay?" Freda offered.

"Thank you Freda. Yes. Gay." Dianna batted her eyes at Kristen who had found her feet.

"Okay," Kristen glanced over her shoulder at her friends as Wesley led her to the main bar. Freda was showing her two enthusiastic thumbs and Dianna was waving at her excitedly.

"How awkward," she breathed.

Wesley turned to her as he handed her the drink and led her to a table in a quiet corner. "What is?"

"Me. Me right this moment," she answered, taking a sip of the heavily coconut flavoured drink.

"No. You couldn't be even if you tried."

She smiled shyly. "So what happened Friday night? With Torea, I mean. You guys seemed to hit it off pretty well."

Wesley made a sound that was close to a snort. "Are you kidding me?" he laughed. "She's a child. I'm pretty sure her publicist had quite an earful from her parents."

Kristen felt relief rushing through her. "Why are you here?" she took a deep drink from the glass.

"I came to see you. I was at the Krimson Kimono and –"

"Nat told you I'd be here?" she interrupted.

She didn't look surprised but she looked slightly expectant, he decided. "No…well yes. I half begged half groveled."

Kristen gave an appreciative laugh. "I would have paid to see that."

"Paid to see me grovel?"

She laughed just a little louder than before. "No. To see Natasha's face *while* you groveled."

Wesley grimaced. "I'm not even going to try to remember it," he said rolling his eyes. "Is it real?" He gestured to her, "The accent."

She nodded. "Yes. I've been to school in London for the greater part of my life."

"But you're originally from Cape Town?" he asked before taking a slug of his drink. He noticed the guarded look that settled over her features.

"No. I'm from Italy. My mum is Russian and my dad is Italian. They met at a market in Italy. Fell in love, had my brother one year later. He was eighteen when they had me."

He noticed the forlorn tone of her voice. "So they must've spoilt you rotten?"

"My mum died giving birth to me. My father traveled a lot and my brother sort of ran the *family business*." She shuddered when she said the word "business".

"I'm sorry to hear about your mum. I'm an only child. No brothers or sisters. My parents married late in life. By the time they had me my dad suffered his first stroke. He can't move his left side very well. By the time I was in high school my dad was still working even though he was medically boarded from work."

Kristen smiled sympathetically. She knew what it was like to feel like an only child. She also knew what it was like having a parent who couldn't give her the attention she yearned for. Though she knew her father and her brother loved her dearly, it was the attention she had seeked the most. She opened her mouth to say something when Freda's voice rang out behind her. "Kristen, darling I hate to do this, but we're going to be off soon."

Dianna was suddenly there beside Freda. "Surely if you want to visit a little longer, Wesley will see that you'll get home safely. Won't you Wesley?"

Before Kristen could protest, Wesley answered, "Of course. She hasn't finished her drink yet."

"Excellent!" Freda dropped a kiss on Kristen's glossy hair. "I'll call you in the morning. And don't do anything I *would*."

"Freda!" Dianna shrieked.

"What?" Freda said as they already moved away. "Did you see the ass on that man?"

Kristen dropped her head in sheer horror, "I'm so sorry."

Wesley drained the last of his drink. "They are talking about *my* ass right?"

"Yes. It is pretty good." She won a laugh from him and echoed it gleefully. After a second round of drinks, Wesley reached for one of her hands. "Where do you live?"

"Wale Street. You know the Mandela Rhodes Place?"

He whistled through his teeth in admiration. "Wow!"

"Is it out of your way? I could always call a cab." She pointed in the general direction of the door.

"No. It's on my way. Well, sort of. I live in the City too. Shortmarket Street near the theatre."

She nodded knowingly, "*On Broadway?*"

"Yes. Is that what it's called?" he teased. He gave her a lingering look. "Do you want to go for a walk?"

"I-I... I can't. But, I'm free for lunch tomorrow... if you'd like to have lunch?"

Wesley smiled. "I'd love to." He watched as she rose from the chair. She was breath taking. He rose himself and led her out to his black VW Golf 5. He opened the door for her, and closed it once she was seated.

Then he got in himself. The music player automatically started to play where it left off. He was concentrating on the traffic and hardly noticed her surprise etched over her features. "What is it?" he asked, steering the car down Main Road toward the city.

"*Mozart?*" she pointed to the source of music.

"Surprised?" he glanced at her.

She was slightly turned towards him with her head resting against the leather seat. Shrugging, she wrinkled her nose. "No. Well, yes. I wasn't expecting Mozart."

"What were you expecting?" he challenged.

"I don't know. Maybe *Nickleback* or *Mean Mr Mustard.*"

"You know *Mean Mr Mustard?*"

"Yes. I think they're pretty good. Did you know that the band is named after John Lennon's cat?"

Wesley nodded thoughtfully. "No I didn't. What kind of music do you like?"

"I love *Radiohead.* You know them?"

Wesley could have sworn that she was beaming. He could see her from the corner of his eye, "So what? Are you like a heavy metal rock chick?"

She rolled her eyes at him, "I like all types of music. I particularly like bands." It felt like five minutes had passed, and she was almost disappointed that he was already taking the bend where Adderley Street became Wale Street. "You can turn right at the first road. Thanks, this is *me.*"

He parked his car and opened the door for her. "I'll walk you up."

There was a slight chill in the air by the time they reached the turnstile entrance of the Mandela Rhodes Place. Wesley turned to her questioningly. "Do you know that – " he pointed to the gray building across the road "– is the Provincial Legislature?"

Kristen laughed as she greeted the neatly dressed doormen. "How are you this evening, Sipho?" She turned and looked back at Wesley. "Yes. Of course I know. I've been here four months."

The elderly man bowed slightly. "I'm well Miss Kristen. I haven't seen you around lately."

Kristen hit the button on the lift. "That's because you've been working the late shift."

He nodded in agreement and waved back at her as the metal doors slid together.

She turned to face Wesley. "I think I had too much to drink."

"In that case I will have to see that you are safe inside your apartment and that you lock up the second I leave."

Kristen was feeling slightly silly, but she couldn't control the flirt that had settled into her head. "Surely you know how to latch the door." Kristen found crazy satisfaction in the way Wesley turned slightly uncomfortable. He was shifting nervously with every step she took closer. It would be the worst idea to kiss him, but there was something about her attraction to him that outranked her moral standards. A few more seconds and she couldn't guarantee that a simple kiss would be all she wanted. Her heart raced like the speed of racehorses at a *met*. She was so deep in her romantic hallucinations that she barely realised Wesley was carrying her out of the lift.

"Which suite are you in?" His breath felt hot against her neck as he spoke.

Kristen's arms stole around his neck and she pressed her forehead against his cheek, "404. It's right here." Her feet barely touched the ground. Reluctantly she fumbled in her bag for her keys, unlocked the door and held it open. She knew she was giving him her most alluring stare. It was one that had a 100% success rate of getting laid. And, though she wasn't the kissing-sleeping-together-on-the-first-date type girl, Wesley was different. There was something special about him that had put her at ease, lower her guard and made her entirely too comfortable with him. She was still hovering in the door with him standing in the hallway outside her apartment. Kristen wondered if the tortured look on his face was because he was mentally restraining himself from touching her or if he was contemplating a quick escape. Do you want to come in for a cup of coffee?" she unbuttoned the first two buttons of her shirt revealing a deep cleavage. It marveled her to see Wesley gape at the sleekness of her skin, but then his eyes locked on hers and a dark look settled over his features before he spoke.

"I should go," he said. "I have a meeting in the morning."

Kristen clutched the sides of her shirt in a desperate apologetic gesture. "I'm sorry, Wesley," she grabbed at his arm as he turned in the direction of the lift. "I wasn't thinking. I never do this."

He didn't look as though he believed her. Had it been any other stranger, she never would have let him into the building, let alone take the lift up to her apartment. What if he thought she was a sleazy tart? What if he didn't show for lunch tomorrow? "We are still on for lunch right?"

Wesley looked her in the eyes. She hoped she didn't look or sound too desperate. How could one night turn into such a disaster? She was in deed the world's cheapest drunk.

"Yes. You just get some sleep," he said, handing her a business card he pulled from his breast pocket.

She shook her head vigorously. "You said you'd make sure I was safe. You said you'd wanted to know I was locked up and safe." She was repeating herself. It was so frustrating. She didn't even realise he was steering her back into her apartment.

"Now lock the door. I want to hear it click."

Kristen gaped at him in disbelief. "You don't want to kiss me do you?"

"Kristen…" he started, but she held a hand out to him to stop. Tears were forming in her eyes, already making him a blur. She nodded in understanding. "It's all right. I get it."

"Kristen? Please don't cry. You don't understand." His voice held a beleaguered plea.

"No Wesley," she cried. "I understand just fine." With that she closed the door.

# CHAPTER THREE

*N1 City, Goodwood, Cape Town*
*Wednesday, 19 March 2008*
*12:00pm*

Lutzio Montello was not a man to be messed around or kept waiting. It would take time for the drug lords or merchants as they were better known as in Cape Town, to grasp. He hated the lax atmosphere. It reminded him of the oblivious parts of India where standing in a line to pee into a hole in a floor in one of the trendiest malls had given him foreign rage. It was also the inspiration of establishing one of the most sought after hotels in India – *Talducci*. It had gone past the two-hour mark and he was now ready to leave the neo-Italian coffee shop that his prospective local business partner and longtime contact had chosen. Lutzio glanced around the cozy little restaurant. It was stuffy. Neat round wrought iron tables and chairs. Crete stone tiles in a deep sandy brown colour graced the floor. A tiny bar close to the entrance with rich dark marble fixtures had artificial greenery strategically placed to lure shoppers. There was nothing Italian about the place except the name and the names of the dishes scribbled in the menu. Full stop. He rolled his eyes as he made a mental note to open a proper Italian coffee shop should he decide that Cape Town had the correct target market or at least potential to develop a target market for his commodities. One thing was certain. The coffee shop had calming abilities. Lutzio was deciding if it was the water dripping fluidly from a water feature in the shape of a lion's head mounted against the wall, or if it was the dark blue sky and stratus cloud formation painted on a dome right above an inside water feature of a pond-and-shoot in the middle of the floor. He was nearing the last of his fourth cup of coffee when he saw the well-dressed Percival Van Sitter approach him from the side. Percival was a burly man such as himself, with coarse dark hair, a moustache and a double chin. He was clutching an A-4 sized black leather satchel and a cream coloured hat with what looked like a purple satin ribbon tacked onto it with bright pink sequins. The cream colour of the hat matched the blazer and pants he wore and the purple shirt was no doubt a link to the ribbon. What a clown he was doing business with, Lutzio snorted. He reached out and shook Percival's outstretched clammy hand.

"It's good to finally meet you Montello. My boys and I have dreamed of this day." Percival's accent sounded thick and slurry – unlike the accents he'd heard from watching the local news channels, or observing around him in the past couple of hours. English must have been this man's second language, and Lutzio was suddenly staggered by the missing fore top teeth in Percival's generous, but gold infested smile.

"Percy," he nodded in greeting and seated himself across his late guest whose collection of thick gold chains and gold signet rings sporting huge dollar signs were almost as distracting as his teeth. Lutzio decided that if Percival didn't come up with a good way of smuggling 5 tons of cocaine into the country, he would remain a buffoon in his mind for years to come. Dollar signs in the ears of a South African? He watched as Percival flirted with a tiny Caucasian waitress dressed in tight black jeans and shirt with a green apron.

"*Hellos* sweetness. A *lekker* cup of coffee *en 'n ontbyt* special. Bring extra *botter en konfyt my* precious." Percival narrowed his eyes and licked a slow thick tongue over his slightly chapped lips. His eyes were shamelessly glued onto the young woman's breasts as she took his order. He grabbed her butt suggestively as she started away from the table nervously. Chuckling, he turned his attention back to the Italian man who was scowling at him disapprovingly.

Lutzio cleared his throat. "If we're going to be doing business you will have to start treating women with some respect Mr Van Sitter. I have a daughter who could be that girl's age and you would lose your right arm if you ever laid a finger on her. That is someone's daughter or even mother. Have you no respect for your own mother?"

Lutzio bored his lethal gaze into Percival that made the younger man flinch.

"I'm ... uh yes." He stammered. "I *respek* my mother." Embarrassed now, he shot a startled look at the male waiter who had brought his coffee.

"Now," Lutzio began after the waiter was out of earshot. "Tell me about your plan. How are we getting the cargo to this factory that you've been talking about?"

Percival's face lit up, "With the help of the Premier of the Western Cape." At the look of Lutzio's confused face, Percival went on to explain exactly what a Premier was and what a Premier did.

"So a Premier runs a province like a president runs a country?" Lutzio nodded in understanding. "Go on."

"Something like that. Every year in the Western Cape we celebrate New Year with the traditional Kaapse Klopse," he pointed to the ribbon in his hat that was now dangling from a spoke of an empty chair beside him. Again, at the questioning raised brow from Lutzio, he went on to explaining the competition.

"So how does this *Klopse* tie into the Premier and the cargo?"

Percival was the picture of confidence as he spoke. "Premier Wilhelmina Langenhoven is a so-called *coloured*. It's a pre-election year and since she has a history on the Cape Flats, she understands the weight of the *coloured* support-base to her Premiership." He gave Lutzio an assessing look as the waiter placed two breakfast specials in front of them and refilled their coffee cups. The young man looked from Lutzio to Percival as he spoke in a similar, but clearer accent than Percival did. "Will you gentlemen have your complimentary juices now or later?"

"Now would be fine," Lutzio gave him a fleeting but polite smile. "And some garlic butter if you have any."

The waiter nodded before leaving the table.

"This conversation is very interesting Percy, do continue."

Percival waited as the juice and the butter arrived. He turned to the waiter. "*Daai sal alles wees vir nou, outjie. I will call you over when* we need you." Percival turned his gaze back to Lutzio who had started eating his breakfast in silence. "There are a lot of Moslem and Christian families involved in the *Klopse* who are also *merts*."

"*Mert*? What is *mert*?" Lutzio shot him a puzzling glance.

Percival chuckled. "It's a short version of *merchant*, Mr Montello. Anyhow, we have to be very quiet about this deal because there is a war going on between drug lords in the Cape and between the drug lords and the Premier's department." He threw his hands up in a gesture that made Lutzio pause. "I know what you are going to ask about the Premier's department. The thing is, Mr Montello. The Premier – although she knows like the rest of the country – is largely responsible for the development and flourishing of local talent and culture. So together with the local MEC for Sport, they donate large cheques to the Carnival's organising committee every year. Now, instead of getting our cut of the *binges* for next year, we can write to the Premier and tell her that we're getting an international sponsor for equipment. We also tell her that we would like to get youngsters off the street by teaching them physics and biochemistry at a lab in Hawston where the factory is." It was fool proof, Percival thought. With his connections in the police and boarder control, the Premier's stamp of approval would get them the manpower for next to nothing, as well as a colossal fortune.

"So then how long will this take if the Carnival is at the beginning of the year? It's almost Easter. Do we have to wait until next year?" Lutzio sounded slightly irritated.

"Mr Montello," Percival leaned over to the older man over his half eaten plate. "My contact is greasing Langenhoven's wheels as we speak. It just so happens that the MEC for Sport has a cocaine addiction and will be more than cooperative to keep that secret. Good old Andile '*Coke-head*' Phosa is an old client of mine. That one we have in the bag. It also helps that I have two men on my payroll at key police stations including the NSRC and coastal patrol."

Lutzio nodded thoughtfully. "How did you get the cargo from Lagos?"

"We've sent pianos to a contact in Nigeria via rail and road. Our guy up there worked his magic and interacted with my good friends in the NSRC, which in turn alerted my contact, the coast guard and safely managed to get the raw cargo safely and securely to Hawston."

"Undetected by the authorities?"

Percival downed his glass of orange juice in three swallows. He slammed the glass down on the table. "Yep! And better yet, the ether arrived in Nigeria from South Korea today. All we need is Langenhoven's stamp of approval to get it into the country."

"What are your reasons going to be to the Premier for needing ether?" Lutzio looked puzzled.

"Kids use ether at primary school labs to do science experiments like turning starch black and many other chemical evidentiary analysis. So we will be teaching street kids all about science to impress the Premier. Of course they will work for us once the media coverage dies down. That way, local sponsors would latch onto the Carnival and then it's a win-win situation. You get your profit. I get my commission. The Carnival gets exposure and sponsorship. The Premier's political party gets votes and the market grows."

Lutzio looked at the young man who was beaming across the table from him. "That is the best idea I've heard in 20 years." He stretched a hand toward Percival. "You did good lad. I think you make a fine young businessman."

Percival gave a deep chuckle and continued eating his breakfast.


*CBD, Cape Town*
*Wednesday, 19 March 2008*
*12:40pm*

It was moving along slowly to lunchtime.

Kristen had opened the sliding door to her balcony to let the fresh air in. It was a particularly windy day. It was kind of day that the gods designed to follow a nasty hangover.

She lay on her back stretched out on a wooden lounger, dressed in a navy satin robe and sunglasses. Her hair was in disarray and caught up with a black hair-biter.

A bottle of lemon-flavoured water stood on the floor beside her alongside a side plate of half-eaten toast with marmite spread.

Kristen felt queasy thinking about her behaviour with Wesley the previous night. The telephone rang in the background and then her mobile – it rang in that fashion since she'd woken up at 10h30. She didn't even mind the traffic noise today.

All she could think about was Wesley.

What if he was put off by the way she practically threw herself at him? She would know for sure if he'd show up for lunch. It didn't even faze her that she had to be at the theatre over an hour ago.

It's not like she needed the money.

She needed to disappear.

Kristen thought about going to *Krimson Kimono*, but decided against it. A run in the Company Gardens was decidedly a good idea, except the pounding in her head reminded her that sudden movements were a no-go.

Freda always said raw eggs, tomato juice and a dash of vodka was all it took to make a hangover disappear in an instant. The thought of raw eggs were revolting enough to make Kristen wince.

What was she thinking to drink that repulsive drink last night?

Freda suggested it, so Freda knew exactly how she'd react afterward. The truth and logic of Freda's intention made Kristen laugh despite her headache. She laughed uncontrollably for a good few minutes before she thought about Wesley again. He was gorgeous.

She glanced at the time.

If Wesley didn't make it for lunch, lunch was going to make it to Wesley.

Kristen ignored the pounding in her head as she prepared her outfit and then jumped into the shower. She kept reminding herself that she was in South Africa - Cape Town to be exact.

There was a snowball's chance in hell that her father or her brother would think of finding her in the Mother City.

She loved the new life she'd started. Her new identity meant new avenues to explore. And so it was that Wesley Petersen had found his way into her mind again.

"I am obsessed!" she yelled at the top of her lungs. Hot water soaked her hair as she lathered her herbal shampoo through her long sleek tresses.

Moments later she was draped in a bath sheet.

The day was looking up.

So what if Wesley got the wrong impression of her? It wasn't what he thought of her that mattered.

He was so dispensable. In terms of toys – he was the new 48-paged colouring book and she was the stuffed cuddly bunny that was carried everywhere. She was way higher on the favourite-o-meter by herself.

And, if there was one thing that always made Kristen feel better – no matter what – that required no man, no thinking just reckless desire and crazy tendency. She was ready to start the day.

Kristen went shoe shopping!

## Hout Street, Cape Town
## Wednesday, 19 March 2008
## 13:10pm

It was stuffy as hell. The power had cut out yet again. Wesley was almost certain he wasn't going to make lunch. Although the rolling blackouts meant that he could take a well-deserved break, Wesley also knew that he could be at the office well into the night if the power hadn't come on by 15h30.

It was a moderate day.

He was grateful for his selection of clothes. It seemed more than fitting to be semi-casual today. His camel trousers and short sleeve white linen shirt was lighter than the stuffy suit he wore the day before. Surely his brown loafers made his attire look fit for the office.

Wesley sat with his elbows on his desk and his head propped on his folded hands. The smell of fruit tobacco reached his nostrils. It was a mixture of peach and cherry. Jacques was bound to appear at any moment and Wesley braced himself to say "no" at the request to lend him some money.

"Wesley my *broer*! We get the day off man. Goliath and Marcus said there isn't much we can do." Jacques was already stoned.

Wesley grew up in Mitchell's Plain.

He knew all the tricks in the book. He knew all about smoking crack and mixing it with fruit tobacco. Marijuana was also easily disguised, and Jacques had definitely been smoking pot. His eyes were bloodshot and a thick sheen washed over his face and neck.

Wesley smiled politely. "Thank you, Jacques. But I have some paperwork to file. I think I'll work until after lunchtime."

Jacques rolled his eyes and ran a shaky hand through his hair. "Suit yourself man." He started away from Wesley and was soon stepping into the lift and out of sight.

Wesley reached into the cupboard of his workstation. He was behind with his paper work and had just managed to printout the previous week's statements for their Swedish client. It would be easy if he could work through the hard copy and find the glitch that Daniel Marcus, CEO and technical director, had asked him to find at the morning conference. According to Daniel, there had been complaints by their clients that excessive amounts of money reflected in their accounts at the ATM but the balance after a withdrawal reflected the true amount. It was a strange glitch. It was mind boggling since Vito Goliath; Daniel's partner and systems developer also couldn't quite tally the fault. Wesley sat staring at the figures in front of him when a flash of movement caught his eye in the direction of the door. There didn't seem to be anybody. Maybe, he thought, it was just the trick of the light. He went back to work for a few more minutes when he heard the slight jingle of keys. It came from the direction of the door. Wesley felt his blood freeze over in his veins. He was certain he was alone. He listened again. Nothing. He let out a deep sigh. He wasn't paranoid. Not in the least, but the sudden unease was making his skin prickle. He rose quickly at the sound of shuffling. It could be his imagination, but someone seemed to be breathing behind him. Then with the force of a ton of bricks, an object collided with the back of his head and all was black.

They weren't letting anyone into the building in Lower Hout Street. Kristen looked up at the five-storey building. She'd just entered the building and was about to sign her name onto he visitor's log page when the entry security guard told her the building was going to be evacuated. She still had the two white takeaway bags in her hand hoping that she would spot Wesley instantly as he came out of the building. He never came out of the building. After half hour, there was still no-show. This was ridiculous. It had been an hour and surely Wesley couldn't have been working in the dark. Kristen turned to the guard who had stopped her from signing the register. She was about to ask him if everyone was out when an eccentric-looking man in a board shorts, a vest and flip-flops stumbled down the stairs. "Help! Help!" he shouted hysterically. "There's been a break-in and I think Wesley is still in there!"

Kristen felt her heart drop into her bottomless stomach. The bags dropped from her hands. Two cops in city patrol vans stopped in front of the building. Both got out – hands on their guns as they made their way up the stairs, which *eccentric-incarnate* had come. Kristen risked a glance at him. He was sitting on the pavement just outside the door of the building. His sling bag was flung open. She took a few steps closer to observe the weird scenario. He took out a cellphone and punched in a number. Kristen wasn't close enough to hear what he was saying, but the shock and turmoil he expresses seconds ago, was now replaced by instant gratification. He was still on the phone when his eyes locked on hers. He froze for a second, and then he said something she did hear. "It's all set. It's just a matter of time. Just a statement."

Kristen shook the images from her head. What could that have possibly been about?

She hadn't even realised that a team of paramedics had entered the building until they came out with a swaying and confused Wesley.

"Oh my God! Wesley!" she ran to him, but an arm stole around her waist. It was one of the cops. His nameplate read: CLARKE. The voice that came from his mouth was a calm, easy and clear one. A soothing one. "It's okay. He will be all right, ma'am. Were you in the building?"

Kristen tensed. She turned to look at the handsome cop. His blue eyes sparkled in his delicately sculpted face. He was young and had the look of an innocent schoolboy, but the muscular arm around her waist told her he was no boy.

"No. No I wasn't in the building." She adjusted the strap of her bag. "We were supposed to meet for lunch. I came by a little earlier to surprise him," her voice trailed off. Then she added glumly, "I was in the foyer, so technically I was in the building." Then, as if remembering something important, she whipped her head back to the eccentric-incarnate on the sidewalk. He now held the same shocked expression he had stumbling out the building about twenty minutes before. Clarke's voice made her blink, "Ma'am? Are you alright?"

"Yes. I just had a terrible fright." Kristen's eyes locked with Wesley's. It was only then that the smell of grilled chicken and garlic butter reached her. She looked down into the short stretch of road between them. The lunch she'd brought him lay strewn and trampled between them. Her gaze shot back to his. He looked like he was in pain – clutching the back of his head with what looked like an icepack.

"Kristen?" Wesley thought the concussion he suffered had made him hallucinate. The woman of his dreams was standing twenty feet from him with concern etched all over her celestial face. Yes, they had a date. He thought that after last night she might have read his restraint as rejection. Her being here suddenly made him lose the control over his emotion and he let out a cry. Seconds later he was in a soft, feminine embrace. He was being caressed and kissed all over his face by her. Wesley's free hand cupped her face as he gently moved back to study her face again. She was crying too. "I thought I'd lost you! I thought something bad had happened to you and that I'd never see you again. I thought-"

He listened as she rambled. Was it possible that she cared about him this much? He wanted to say: "I'm alright. I was hit in the head with something" but gave in to the overwhelming urge and covered her mouth with his. She hesitated for a second, before he felt her soft warm mouth open in invitation for him to deepen the kiss.

He tasted better than she'd imagined him to. Faint mint and apricot hinted in his kiss. Kristen curled her arms around his neck and gave in to the fluttering sensations in her stomach that seemed to spread to her chest and eventually her head, leaving her dizzy. She swayed as she stepped away from him. She felt a hand seize her wrist and managed to find her balance. It was Clarke. She turned back to Wesley who was now surrounded by paramedics once more.

Despite the splitting headache, Wesley's head was everything but cloudy. He watched Kristen, as she genuinely looked terrified for him and his injuries. The kiss they'd shared was more personal and intimate than he expected. He marveled at the way she molded her curvy body into his in those few seconds that seemed like an eternity. The smell of garlic butter and grilled chicken reached his nose and his stomach rolled, sickened.

"We need to get you to the hospital, son." It was one of the paramedics talking to him. "You are going to need a doctor to take a look at that nasty bump on your head. They might even keep you for a day or two."

Wesley was about to protest, but the zinging in his ears made his head ache even more. He followed the paramedic to the ambulance where Kristen climbed in beside him.

# CHAPTER FOUR

*Greenpoint, Cape Town*
*Wednesday, 19 March 2008*
*14:30pm*

Natasha looked around her. There was a high demand for pickled fish this time of the year. Since the tourist season seemed to be prolonged, she altered the menu to match Holy Week. Yes, it was ridiculous how modern Christians always seemed to "give up" something for Lent. If it wasn't smoking, it was alcohol or chocolate. Meat on the other hand seemed to be an all-round no-no during this most spiritual season. The change in their menu seemed to attract a slightly older generation and the health conscious political crowd. Today, the Premier was having a luncheon meeting with a very exotic looking gentleman and an obvious local wannabe thug. Natasha rolled her eyes at the American influences published by the media that put all kinds of creative dressing ideas into the minds of local Cape Flats inhabitants.

The fish platter and roasted vegetables was taken to the Premier's table. Wilhelmina Langenhoven was a striking woman in her mid-50s. Her coarse chemically treated hair was a rich shade of brown with auburn highlights. Her thin, oval face was expertly made up with obvious high quality makeup that left a smooth, airbrushed look about her. The white embroidered collar and sleeve hems added an elegant hint to the black suit that would otherwise be seen as professional. Thick gold hoops graced her ears and a matching gold necklace sat high above her defined collarbones. If there was one woman in local politics that deserved to be on the cover of a fashion magazine, it was Wilhelmina Langenhoven.

By the looks of the Italian-looking man dinning with her, they were talking about business. Natasha saw something familiar in his features that she couldn't quite pin to where she'd seen him before, but she knew it would hit her at some point. Just then, the phone rang. It was Kristen calling from the hospital.

"Are you okay? What happened?" Natasha gasped.

"I'm fine, Nat. It's Wesley. The guy you gave my schedule to."

Natasha let out a breath. "You aren't upset are you?" She heard Kristen give a weary laugh on the other end.

"No not at all. On the contrary actually. We had a drink after the show. He took me home. We made plans for lunch. When he didn't call, I went over to his work only to find that there was a blackout in that part of town. I thought he was held up for some reason. Instead he was nearly bludgeoned to death."

Natasha drew in a shaky breath. "Is he okay?"

"Yes. Just a concussion and a bruised cheek, but otherwise, he is fine. He has to stay for observation, so I'll only be in on Friday."

"I thought we were going to close early Friday afternoon."

"Nat, I meant you could take off early Friday night and I'll lock up. In fact, we are closed from Saturday. Tell the staff the Krimson Kimono will be open from Tuesday."

Natasha yawned in spite of herself, "Yep. Do you want me to make up a platter for you and, I assume, your new boyfriend."

Kristen gave an appreciative laugh. "No thanks. I'll just nuke him some chicken soup."

"Whatever you say boss lady. I have to go. You will never believe who chose us as a luncheon destination."

"Who?"

Natasha could hear the anxiety in Kristen's voice, and decided to take the suspense away, "Premier Wild and Wacky Wilhelmina Langenhoven."

"You are shitting me!"

"Nope. I have to go collect a nice fat tip."

Kristen laughed and hung up. She walked back into the tiny but comfortable hospital room where Wesley lay asleep against the crisp white pillows. His face seemed relax despite the trauma earlier that day. It was going to be one Easter that she was sure going to enjoy. What had Natasha said about him being her boyfriend? Kristen sighed in delight. The prospect of having Wesley as her boyfriend felt good. She went closer and sat down beside him on the bed. Suddenly exhausted, she kicked off her shoes and curled up against him.

## Christiaan Barnard Memorial Hospital, Cape Town
## Thursday, 20 March 2008
## 02:20am

The delicious heat that spread beside him gave Wesley the confirmation that he was not alone on the hospital bed. The pounding in his head had subsided, but was still weighing his head down. He moved a lazy hand over a feminine curve. An action that won him a sleep induced murmur. He strained to see the sight that made his lungs burn and the bottom of his stomach drop out.

Kristen was curled up in a ball with her arms tucked into her drawn up knees and her head resting on his chest. Her naked arms felt slightly cool. The way she nuzzled her lush body against him sent the clean floral scent of her surrounding his senses. The light from the corridor was dimmed and the door was opened a jar that gave enough light for him to check the time on the round clock beside the door.

It was just after 3am.

Wesley wasn't sure for how long he was out. But the regrowth of beard told him not longer than a day. Kristen stirred again and strained against him. Instinctively he pulled her closer to him. He listened to the difference in her breathing, and as if sensing his concern, she reached out for his face. "I'm awake," she murmured and stretched out like a spoilt kitten.

Wesley watched as she pulled the covers away from him slowly and then settled even closer to him, yet careful not to move the mattress too much. The intense heat of her body and the scent of her sent a painful stirring in his groin. She was still dressed in the same black spanks and royal blue tennis dress. The powder blue hospital gown was the only separation between her roving hand and his chest.

"Does your head hurt when you move it at all?" her voice was barely a whisper.

Wesley turned his head slightly to look down into her wide eyes where he found concern and fear. It was pooled there until he noticed a deep stirring of another emotion that made his heart bang in his chest. "Kristen…" before he could utter another word she was kissing him ever so softly. He stole a hand under the dress and ran a hand up and down her back. Her skin was warm and soft. She felt like a ripe peach beneath his touch. His body tensed out of its own accord as she deepened their kiss. Her fingers were locked in the curling mass of his hair.

The same hand that moments ago soothed her back was now peeling one of the sleeves down her porcelain shoulder. His lips brushed the side of her mouth before traveling to her cheek and the underside of her jaw. The rapid pulse at the base of her neck made for an interesting metronome for his flickering tongue. Her breath was hot against his ear. It came in shallow puffs as her fingers dug into his shoulders. He brushed his lips along the slender length of her neck. His soft heated kiss set her skin ablaze beneath his lips. The choked moans she tried to bite back were the cause of sheer pleasure.

She trembled beneath his searching hand. He pulled her closer to his body. Her response told him that she was eager for him to explore more of her. One of her shapely legs hiked up and over his lap. Wesley kissed his way back to her sweet mouth where he lingered before Kristen came up for air. Even in the dark, he could see the flare of colour on her cheeks. She was beautiful. Her big eyes sparkled in the moonlight and it took his breath away. Wesley ignored the pounding in his head. He was lost in the swirling green depths of Kristen's eyes. Her slightly parted lips were kiss-swollen perfection that glistened in invitation to be kissed again. Her roaming hand slid timorously down his smooth ripped abdomen until it settled quivering over his engorged penis. Wesley's eyes closed at the feel of her flesh on his most sensitive being. Her hand trembled slightly but she didn't move it. He opened his eyes to find her looking at him questioningly. "I don't want you to hurt anywhere," she whispered; her voice laced with tears. "I was so scared Wesley. When you didn't come out of that building... I thought... I thought..." she shook her head as though she could rid herself of the image that he knew she saw in her head. It could not have been a pleasant one by the sudden terror edged in her features.

"It's okay Kristen. I'm here. *We* are here together. It was just rotten luck."

Kristen was beside herself. Her eyes burned with stubborn tears that she tried to blink away. The moment gave her a clear view of her position. She was sitting astride Wesley. Her legs were somehow wrapped around his waist and the pillow that rested behind his neck on the inclined bed were scattered on the floor. Her one hand rested on his shoulder and the other was casually draped over his naked erection. The feel of his flesh burning and throbbing against her hand added hot moisture to the throbbing between her thighs. His hands were on her shoulders as he spoke; stroking and pushing the sleeves of her dress further down her arms until her the cool night air caressed her nakedness where it disappeared at the bunched dress around her hips.

She watched as his eyes traveled down to where her hair tumbled over her shoulders to her elbows. He brushed the silken mass from her shoulders and cupped the firm heaving breasts that sent her blood soaring in her veins. The gentle molding of his hands bought forerunners of a greater promised pleasure to her core. When he sought out her mouth, his kiss was deep and urgent enough to make Kristen moan his name in sheer ecstasy.

The sound of his name rolling off her tongue drew the primal sexual male eagerness from Wesley. Despite his moral beliefs, Kristen had some power over him that made him want her right there in his hospital cot. Moments later he was removing the bunched dress and the elastic spanks from her legs with her panties in one fluid movement. Her nakedness was that of perfection. Her luscious curves were calling out to him.

Kristen reached for him and tugged the blue hospital gown from his shoulders. She couldn't think past the pleasure that would unfold when Wesley took her. He was having trouble lowering his weight on her as though the effort was causing him pain. Despite the need burning inside her, Kristen heard herself say, "We can wait for this, love."

*Love.*

A word that triggered something inside him like a trapdoor in his heart sucking him in and making him fall into a bottomless room filled with rose petals. Wesley settled himself between her legs and marveled at her readiness for him. He watched the waves of pleasure on her face as he pushed gently into her.

Kristen bit her bottom lip to prevent from screaming out in rapture. He was stretching her tight core in a painful yet pleasing manner that made her raise her hips for more. He pulled out of her and then entered her with a strong, sure thrust that took the breath out of her.

Kristen felt like liquid velvet around him. He loved the way her legs curled around his waist as she lay beneath him. He moved with even strokes as he thrust deeper and deeper into her with each tantalizing movement. The sound of his name came in a whisper as her entire body quivered beneath him until her body tensed around him before her pleasure broke in wild hot contractions around him. Wesley pulled her up toward his chest as he thrust deeper and faster into her. Her arms tightened around him as his own release knocked them both back down against the inclined bed.

They lay entwined for what felt like half an eternity trying to catch their breath and reduce the thudding of their heartbeats. Wesley pulled the thin hospital sheets up to her neck when the heat of their lovemaking left her body and the cool breeze finally made them both shiver. He curled up next to her. His head throbbing dully as he buried his face in her neck.

Kristen knew she had to get out of bed and get dressed, but her muscles were far too relaxed for her to care. With Wesley's arms securely around her, she welcomed the sleep that was inevitable after the intense sensual physical love he had made to her.

## *Wale Street, Cape Town*
## *Thursday, 20 March 2008*

Her apartment smelt just like her. It was tastefully furnished with clean trimmed detail that was both expensive and universal. The beige, brown, orange and yellow setting of her lounge was inviting. The blinds were still drawn – for which he was grateful as a rush of sunlight introduced to his throbbing head would surely be the death of him.

Wesley laughed silently as he remembered the nurse's face when she walked into his hospital room that morning to find, instead of one but, two naked people in a bed with a bold all cap notice above the bed that read: NIL PER MOND. He turned to the sound of the door closing behind him. Kristen stood in the door viewing him intently. "Why do you look like a cat that got the cream?" she asked with an anticipating smile. She walked further into the lounge with her handbag and a medium pull-along suitcase they'd collected from Wesley's flat after they left the hospital.

"I was just thinking about last night." He sat down on an overstuffed suede two-seater, stretching his legs in front of him.

She blushed shyly as she remembered just how that memory went. It included the shocking penetration that woke her. He had taken her from behind and she had enjoyed the helplessness she felt when he brought her to her peak and she climaxed in breathlessness. And, again as dawn broke in crimson and orange ribbons the slow manner of his lovemaking had her in tears of sweet joy. And just as he had let the cover fall to the ground the fourth time, the young blonde nurse had dropped her medication tray and went three shades paler than white wash when she saw the rather peculiar sexual knot Kristen and Wesley had been molded into.

Kristen released the breath she'd been holding and then burst out laughing. The uncontrollable fit of laughter had Wesley on his feet and beside her. His arms stole around her, "Is it too soon to tell you that I love you?"

She smiled up at him, "Not at all."

"Then I love you." He kissed her lightly when the telephone rang right beside him. The sound made him cringe and hold his head.

Kristen picked up the phone and covered the mouthpiece. "I'm so sorry. The bathroom is that way," she pointed down a passage, "it's the last door on the right."

He winked at her as he made his way down the dimly lit passage.

Kristen cleared her throat before she spoke. "Kristen Katts."

"What the hell happened to you yesterday? We were so worried! I called your phone over and over and I wasn't sure if I had to report you missing." Dianna's voice came in a high-spirited squeak. "Kristen?"

"I'm here. I was at the hospital."

Dianna sounded a little confused when she spoke again. "Are you okay? What happened?"

"You remember the guy on Tuesday night at the show?"

"Wesley? Yeah, how did that go? And what the hell were you doing in hospital? Are you okay?"

Kristen rolled her eyes. "I had a lunch date with Wesley. I wasn't at the theatre in the morning because of the hangover I suffered from the night before."

Dianna giggled and allowed Kristen to finish the story. By the end of Kristen's tale, having left out the censored bits, Dianna cooed. "Deeeeeelightful! Not the bit where he was almost bludgeoned to death, but the romantic gesture."

Kristen smiled into the phone. "Yes well. The conclusion is that I brought him back here from the hospital. He is off work for the next week. I'm going to be taking care of him."

Dianna gasped. "Is that wise? You hardly know him."

"Hey!" Kristen teased. "You and Freda will be to blame if he turns out to be a psycho with some contagious disease." Suddenly, her own words made her blood turn to ice. Wesley. They hadn't used a condom.

Wesley let the water run over his tense shoulders. He felt remorse at washing the smell of Kristen from him. He did, however, take comfort in the fact that he was in her apartment and for the next week he would have her around him all the time. He turned off the taps and reached for a white terrycloth robe. He toweled his hair dry and left the bathroom. She was still on the telephone when he strode into the lounge. The stricken horror on her face froze him in his stride. His mind raced. He watched anxiously as she put the receiver back in the cradle. "Kristen? Is something wrong?"

"I just realised that we didn't use anything last night."

The look on her face squeezed at his heart. "Kristen? What is your concern?" Searching her eyes, he asked in a softer tone, "Are you afraid of falling pregnant? I mean, if you are, we could-"

"It's not that!" she exclaimed. "I've never slept with anyone without protection." She looked genuinely freaked out.

"I'm clean. I don't have any sexual transmitted diseases or infections."

She released a shaky breath. "Neither do I."

Wesley noticed that she was still tense even though she did relax a notch. "We could get tested if you like. Is there something else bothering you?"

"Yes. I have to go to the Krimson Kimono. I need to pick up some of my things. I also have a show tonight. It's the one thing that I can't get out of. I'm playing a solo. It also happens to be the one that I didn't practice for."

Wesley's brows drew together in a dark scowl. "*Playing* a solo?"

"I play the guitar in the *Music Man* at the Artscape Theatre. It's the first show of three shows, starting tonight."

## The Krimson Kimono, Greenpoint., Cape Town
## Thursday, 20 March 2008

There was quite a flow of odd characters streaming into the Krimson Kimono in one day, Natasha reflected as the wannabe gangster lingered after the burly big shot and the Premier had gone their separate ways. He was ogling the *Yoko* as Charlie's Angels just started their shift. After eating most of the dishes on the menu, Natasha had waltzed over to his table out of sheer inquisitiveness. "You some kind of agent, boyo?"

Percival Van Sitter looked up at her in surprise. After taking in her physique, he flashed a gold infested smile. "*Hoe lyk dit*? Me'n you girl." He bobbed his head at her suggestively.

Natasha grimaced. "I'm sorry. I don't date clients." At least not scaly ones, she added silently. Natasha heard him curse under his breath, but continued on her way to a couple at the far end of the restaurant who waved her over. By the time she'd scribbled their order down, she turned back to find that the thug was now joined by a tall sophisticated strawberry blonde in a gray linen suit and pink silk shirt. Her bold silver accessories broke the otherwise secretary look. She peered at him over her frameless spectacles. She seemed to be in her early to mid forties. Natasha could hear the heavy accented English as she took notes as the local thug tried his best to use simple English.

His efforts were hilarious! Natasha found herself needing to escape into the kitchen every so often to let rip a hysterical laugh.

### *Wale Street, CBD, Cape Town*
### *Thursday, 20 March 2008*

"How's your head?"

"It's okay. Feels a heck of a lot better than it did a few hours ago," Wesley smiled down at Kristen as he dried the dishes she'd been washing in the fitted kitchen. "I think the fact that the hospital smelt like *hospital* and the food was just as tasty as cardboard were major factors in intensifying my headache."

Kristen laughed. "I hope lunch wasn't half as bad."

"Not at all," he said with a wink. "It's not everyday that the most beautiful woman in the world serves you cheese spread toast with lettuce and tomato."

She jabbed a dripping finger in his direction as she spoke. "I didn't realise I was out of real cheese. You did ask for a cheese sandwich. You didn't say in which form the cheese should be."

After they'd cleaned the kitchen, Wesley swallowed down his medication. "I need to use your telephone."

"No problem. I'm just going to get ready before I have to leave."

He watched her glide down the hallway before he punched his parent's home number.

His mother had answered the phone. She'd told him they were all packed and ready to leave. His friend Alan was picking them up as arranged. They would depart from Cape Town International at 07:05AM and arrive at Johannesburg International at 09:05. It would be the first time that they travel by airplane and the first time that they'd be out of the Western Cape. He'd told his mother that he would not be at his flat for the entire weekend, but he would keep in touch with them once they were settled in their hotel. His cellphone had gotten lost during the commotion the previous day. After listening to the long to-do list his mum rattled off the top of her head, she took a deep breath. "I love you son. Take care of yourself."

"I always do mum. I love you and dad too." Then he heard his mother hang up. The strumming of the guitar made Wesley inquisitive as he followed the sound. The moment he knocked on her room's door, the playing stopped. She called out for him to enter.

"Whoa!" Wesley took in his surroundings with deliberate slowness. The room was dressed up in black and white accessories. Every kind of imaginable guitar was either plugged into a multi-jack or leaned against the wall. Smaller ones were displayed on the walls. There were about sixty-eight guitars in her room. They differed in colour, make and style, but the collection was impressive. Famous musicians signed some and others had dates engraved on them. "I didn't know you were this much of a fan."

Kristen looked smug sitting in the middle of her bed. She had changed into cutoff denims and a sports jacket. The guitar she had laying in her lap was a gorgeous piece of equipment. "My father started buying me a guitar for every time he'd said I'd never be a musician."

There was a sad look in her eyes when he sat down on the bed, "A guitar? That's weird."

She laughed at the memory. "You know how some people say 'I wish I had a penny for every time I heard' something?" She watched him nod before she said, "I said to him that I wish I had a guitar for every time he said I could never be."

"How many are there?"

"Altogether there are one-thirty-two. I got them in a period of two years."

Wesley's eyebrows shot up in surprise. "Damn!"

Kristen tested the strings, playing a few cords. "This one was signed by Bryan Adams. In 2002, my dad had it signed at his concert in Germany. He was there on business, and happened to pull some strings."

Wesley was gaping at her, "*The* Bryan Adams?"

"Yes. I also have some signed my Cheryl Crowe, Jonathan Butler, Ernie Smith and Jimmy Dludlu, and Carlo Santana."

"Jimmy Dludlu?"

"Yeah."

Wesley nodded in fascination. "My dad is a big fan."

*His* family.

It was the second biggest topic next to marriage.

Kristen prayed that he wouldn't ask her to meet his family.

Instead, he told her that he'd sent his parents away for the weekend. Wesley spoke so freely about his past and his life growing up in a coloured community and his personal strife to break the social mold and stereotype associated with young coloured men. His open despise of the crime factor in province made Kristen feel the blow of her own lies. There was no way that she could tell Wesley about her life. What would he think of her if he learnt that she was raised with blood money? People died and families suffered under her father and his business ventures that crippled economies.

She took a deep breath to try and steady her racing heart. This time it wasn't pounding out of desire, but it pounded out of fear. She didn't have to deliberate about the way she felt about Wesley.

She loved him.

He loved her. They'd established that today. Even though they'd been strangers up until a few days ago, she was certain about her feelings.

The attraction was mutual.

They'd made love for crying out loud!

The thought made her blush deeply.

"And that look?" he asked. "Did I say something?"

Kristen shook her head, no. "I was just remembering the nurse in the hospital..." No more words needed. He met her gaze. She was still embarrassed.

"Do you want to talk about that?" he asked.

Kristen shook her head again. "Tell me more about where you grew up. Why do you want to get your folks out of Mitchell's Plain?"

"The crime situation tied together with the drug situation and the unemployment rate.

"There are girls – kids – scholars – who walk around pregnant, smoking and on a drug high.

"Those same kids and their parents blame the government for the way the Cape Flats deteriorated over the past two decades, but that's not the case. These people are making themselves instruments of these social breakdowns." He ran his fingers through his hair. "I grew up on the Cape Flats. I've made something of myself, Kristen.

"When my parents were put out of their home in Goodwood in the 1960's, they were on a waiting list – given a flat in the Maccassar area in the 1980's. It wasn't going to work. They lived with my mother's family for seven years before my father started building on the plot my grandfather had left him.

"My mother worked at an insurance company as a clerk, and my father worked as a bricklayer for a big construction firm. Their blood, sweat and tears over seven years finished our house that my dad built with his own two hands."

This was something Wesley felt strongly about. Earning honest money. Honest money gave one pride, he was telling her.

"It might not make you rich, but it brings you wealth."

Kristen shot him a perplexed look. "What? You just said the same thing."

Wesley made a sound that wasn't quite a snort. "No, it means two different things. Riches don't necessarily mean wealth." Clearly Kristen didn't understand. He tried again. "It's like murder and kill.

It doesn't necessarily mean the same thing. Murder is something that is done intentionally. Whereas killing is something that may happen unintentionally like when you have a fight and you kill someone in self-defense."

Now he was making sense. She thought for a while. "So being rich means that one has a lot of money and worldly riches; where being wealthy means you have plenty to be grateful for like pride, love and happiness?"

Wesley grinned at her. "Something like that," he pulled her into his arms and kissed her thoroughly.

She wanted to lay there with him all day – just burying her face in his neck. His kisses were setting her aflame. His hands felt warm and gentle where he caressed the smoothness of her back until the default tone of her cellphone pulled Wesley away from her.

"Kristen Katts." She listened to Natasha's voice on the other end.

"Kris, you need to get down here right now. There was a delivery for you. Looks like a suit of some kind. It was sent over by," a clinking of zippers and a rustle of nylon sounded before Natasha spoke again. "It was sent over by someone called Siraaj Reddy."

"Thank you. I'll pick it up in a bit."

Natasha gave a weary sigh on the other end. "This has been a very exciting day at the Krimson Kimono."

"How so?"

"Let me rather not get into the details. All I can say is that something really strange is going on. There is a guy here who has been meeting with everyone from the Premier, to the MEC of Sport, to a very exotic foreigner and now he is chatting to a very pristine looking doll."

Kristen laughed. "Maybe he is from a charity organisation."

"Yeah right. The kind of charity where you leave your bag unattended for a second and he'd think you were giving it to charity."

"Nat, I have to go. I'll see you within the hour, okay?" Kristen heard Natasha say her goodbyes before she hung up.

Wesley looked at her questioningly. She could tell that he'd heard everything Natasha had said since the woman did speak loud enough.

Kristen propped herself up on one arm. She was weak with gratefulness that Natasha hadn't called her *boss lady* as the older woman usually had.

"So," Wesley backed away from the bed. The blazing heat she'd seen in his eyes had faded to a tepid flame. "Who is Siraaj Reddy?"

Kristen studied him for a second. "Is that your jealous face?" she laughed after a few moments when it was clear that he wasn't going to answer her. "Siraaj Reddy is an actor who also happens to be directing *The Music Man*."

Wesley nodded feeling silly suddenly. "I'm sorry, it's just..."

He didn't finish the sentence, and she didn't let him either. She smiled up at him, grabbing the guitar from the bed. "This one," she motioned to the instrument in her hands, "belonged to my mother. My dad said she bought it the day she learned she was going to have me. She only listened to Patty Smyth during her pregnancy and she believed that if she kept up an obsession with guitars, I'd become a musician someday."

Wesley listened to the sadness in her voice. It was carried through the sad tune she subconsciously played on the guitar.

"She wanted a little girl. My dad used to tell me that my brother had a sense for business since he was five years old." She rolled her eyes. And, instead of continuing, she gave him a weary smile. "I should get going."

"I have to let my friends know I'm okay."

"You could call from the telephone. It isn't a problem." She dropped a kiss on the top of his head before going into the adjoining bathroom and left Wesley in her bedroom inspecting the crazy guitar collection a bit closer.

## The Krimson Kimono, Greenpoint., Cape Town
## Thursday, 20 March 2008

Kristen waltzed into the Krimson Kimono. She was on a natural high, since Wesley stood waiting for her with a bath sheet when she'd turned off the shower. He had kissed her for good luck, but there desire for each other had bloomed from that one kiss that led to an hour of blissful, sensual physical love. Again he had told her how crazy he was about her. Kristen could hardly believe her luck. Though, she thought about the way she was lying to Wesley by not telling him about her life. About her past... About her family... Somerset Road was bumper to bumper with traffic. The drawn out drive had dampened her spirits just a bit, but then, the memory of him turning the shower open and dragging her back into the little cubical with him had tinged her cheeks hot pink. She practically had to beg Wesley not show up at the theatre tonight. She knew from the night he'd been at the Stuffed Pineapple that she would never be able to concentrate if she knew he was watching her. It was different when she sat on her bed and strummed her guitar though.

She glanced around the restaurant to get a glimpse of the crowd. It had picked up a wee bit. She instantly spotted the "urban gangster" like Freda had labeled the local thugs. Though, Dianna – sweet little Dianna – would simply use the word "coolio". No doubt about it. The woman sitting opposite him was clearly as uncomfortable in his company as the clothes he was wearing. She had her back to Kristen, but the familiarity of her aura set alarm bells off in her head. A hand on her shoulder made her jump. "Damnit!"

"Sorry." Natasha frowned at her. "You okay?"

"Yeah. Just came to pick up the suit."

Natasha handed her the nylon bag. "Good luck tonight. We still closed tomorrow?"

"Yes. And thanks. I'll probably just have to check on the freezers and the geyser tomorrow night, but everything is still good."

Natasha glanced passed her. "You get going, I think the beauty and the beast are done with their meeting."

Kristen gave a brief nod and an air kiss before she dashed out the door.

Natasha turned her attention back to the beautiful woman in her linen suit.

"The bill is for Mr Van Sitter's entire day," her thick British accent had Natasha fumbling for her wits for a few seconds.

"Not a problem," the manager said as she accepted a platinum Swedish bank business account card from the woman. The name read *Dr Anne Thomas, Montello Inc.* Natasha swiped the card and handed the terminal to Dr Anne Thomas.

The 'Dr' signed the slip looking up at Natasha. "The young woman who was just here now, who is she? She looks awfully familiar."

Natasha verified the signature on the back of the card and handed it back to the prissy doctor. "Ms Katts. She comes in when the boss needs her to be here. I'm sure you must be confusing her with someone else."

"Does Ms Katts have a first name?"

"Yes. It's Kristen, actually. Maybe you've seen her at the local theatres?" Natasha saw something dark stir in the strawberry blonde's eyes. It was a strange combination of confusion and acknowledgement that made Natasha raise a questioning brow, "Make a connection?"

"Yes. In a very big way," she bobbed her head to the man beside her. "Someone will be in touch with you for a full report of the weekend's trial run."

Van Sitter nodded, and then with a sleazy smile, he walked out the Krimson Kimono dragging his right leg in a fashioned stroll.

Natasha opened her mouth to ask the doctor if there was anything else she wanted, when the phone rang beside the cash register. She turned to *Ling* who had just stepped through the swing door of the kitchen with a notepad and a pen. She gestured with her index finger between the two women before turning her back and answering the telephone.

Dr Thomas smiled at the geisha-like waitress as she neared her. "Ling?"

"That's right."

"I need your help," Dr Thomas took several bills from her designer purse and fanned it in the waitress's direction. "I think you'd be able to help me with an address."

# CHAPTER FIVE

## Club Galaxy, Athlone, Cape Town
### Thursday, 20 March 2008
### 21h50pm

Wesley knew from the moment he stepped out from the passenger seat of Alan's car that he should never let the boys have talked him into coming to Galaxy tonight, mild concussion and all. Cape Town's oldest, and most popular club was buzzing with youngsters all looking to let their hair down and boogie the night away. Somehow, despite agreeing to it, Wesley couldn't stop thinking about Kristen who was in the city playing her guitar in a fundraising event. She was the most incredible person he'd ever met. The very thought of her sent an uncomfortable stirring in his groin. He was in love, and this time, there was a girl who felt the same about him. No lies. No faking. Just open honesty and trust. His head ached, but Alan had promised that they'd leave by midnight.

"Man," Alan's slouch told Wesley his friend was about to sulk. "Where the hell is your cell? I tried calling you! Has Dylan told you about this chick he's been seeing for the past four months?"

Wesley shook his head, no.

Alan shrugged as he walked to the back of a line forming outside the club in College Road, Athlone. "Apparently that's what he's been doing each time he left us in the lurch." Alan rolled his eyes theatrically and snorted. "*What*. I meant to say '*who*'." He turned to Wesley then who was standing beside him – his black leather jacket slung over his shoulder. Alan glanced around them to see the engrossed gazes raking Wesley who had been as unconcerned as ever. "How do you do it Wes?"

Wesley spared his friend a puzzled glance before checking the time on his wristwatch. "How do I do what?"

"How do you manage to brush off," he motioned to a couple of perfect young women, "that?"

Wesley shrugged. "I guess because I always knew that I'd find my perfect match someday, and I have."

Alan stared up at his friend, peering over his spectacles. "Oh spare me! Please don't tell me that you have secretly been romancing your dream girl and will soon be proposing as well?"

"Not really, but I'm well on my way to proposing." Wesley tapped Alan on the shoulder and watched as the slighter man ran a few feet to catch up with the rapidly moving crowd.

Helgar Swain sat on the lounger just off the main dance floor. She tilted the tumbler that held her all time favourite vodka and lemonade. The ice was already melting as she took a sip. She hated waiting on her boyfriend. They'd met while she was a rookie journalist working for a Southern Suburbs community newspaper. He'd agreed to do a safety column once a month, and seven years down the line, is still her most reliable contact. The last five years had taken their relationship beyond professional boarders and into the category of lovers.

Captain Kieran Clarke - *SAPS*. The thought of him brought a lazy smile to Helgar's full natural pout. Her signature dramatic bold shades of eyeshadow were carefully applied in bright shades of sheer neon green and pink. A thick application of black eye pencil brought out her big bright green eyes. Her oval shaped face was framed by an array of flaming red and blonde frizzy curls. She stuck a cigarette between her glossy burgundy lips. Knowing Kieran - or Clarke, as so many people had called him – he would show up close to midnight. She sighed. The DJ had selected the best club anthems and it seemed that everybody who was everybody was shaking their moneymakers on the crowded dance floor.

Again, Helgar sighed. She would love to be there right now, rubbing up against her guy. It had been weeks since they'd made love. She was working crazy shifts, and so was he. Tonight, however, was the first of five days' leave that she had taken. Thank heavens for her editor who *actually* checked the shift roster and grew a conscience. There was no way that Helgar could possibly pull another fourteen-hour shift from 10pm until 12pm for another week. Five weeks of doing that was becoming hell. Not that the night allowance wasn't worth every penny, but damned if she suddenly passed out behind the wheel of her car.

She rolled her shoulders and flexed her neck. She needed to unwind. She was still tense. It was weird how a journalist could never just chill out. She had long since jumped ship from the community newspaper to one of Cape Town's biggest daily newspapers. Kieran had a habit of calling her a cyborg. He teased her about setting eyes on someone and having their entire files from their blood type to the colour and fabric of their underwear displayed in her digital-slash-x-ray vision. Right now, that seemed to be almost spot-on as *Hailey Langenhoven, 22, Law Student – UWC, daughter and only child of Premier Wilhelmina Langenhoven, undercover tikkop and floozy,* swayed passed her – drink in hand – with her usual classy, but flashy friends. Flashy in the *fleshy* sense.

Helgar grimaced.

The girls circled around Hailey were known among the media circles as the *Lollipop Gang* due to their unfailing outros of their evenings with *tik* lollies. Crystal Methamphetamine aka *Tik* was killing off brain cells of the next generation of would-be lawyers. Helgar gave a mental shrug. It seemed to her that every profession had its preferred social drug. Yes, well, there were so many of her colleagues and distant colleagues who sort the aid of marijuana cigarettes as a stress relief. The hypocritical and illusive industry that was journalism in her opinion was a joke to some degree. Helgar took another sip of her drink and shifted her attention to the two men who had set their bottles of beer on a high round table. Both men leaned casually against the chrome tabletop facing toward the dance floor. They were opposite in their appearance. The guy on her left was tall, dark and handsome. She could tell by his exposed forearms that his muscles were defined. His black hair was sleeked back.

For some reason, his mystique was appealing since it was clear that he wasn't *talent* scouting.

His friend, on the other hand, was lanky and shorter. His bright red hair and freckled face could have been cute had his eyes not scanned the club like an anxious deer. His body language alone spoke volumes of desperation. His baggy denim jeans were an obvious bad choice, let alone the long sleeve gray shirt had dark half-moons under the armpits. With the top two buttons undone, the man looked like he would ejaculate if a scantily dressed teenager brushed passed him in a slinky snakeskin dress and heels.

On the walls around the club, plasma televisions were all tuned to *the free channel's* muted late soft porn movie.

Above the blaring music Helgar could hear the *Lollipop Gang* laughing. She turned in their direction just as a warm hand touched her naked shoulder. She didn't have to look behind her to know that Kieran was standing with a coke in one hand and a gorgeous smile. His cologne settled over her senses and set her heart racing. His lips were cold from his drink as he kissed the underside of her jaw. She lifted her jacket and her bag from the lounger, and he took up the empty seat.

"I've missed you," his voice crackled. "How long has it been?"

"It's been more than a month my darling. Four weeks, 5 days and about 10 hours give or take," she gave him a nonchalant roll of her brilliant eyes before he laughed. He started to tell her something when the two men she'd seen earlier on stood right in front of them.

The handsome mysterious man stuck a hand out to Kieran. "Captain Clarke?"

Kieran rose to his feet and shook hands with the two men, "Wesley Johnson." Kieran smiled at the mysterious man. "How's the head?"

Wesley touched his head subconsciously, "Still got the aches, but it's all good."

Kieran turned his attention to the man beside Wesley. "I'm Clarke."

"Superman?" the freckled faced man said animatedly before belching out a laugh. "Sorry, sorry!" he touched a hand to his stomach, then to his head before shaking Kieran's hand.

Kieran politely smiled at him, "That was rather funny —"

"Alan," the redhead said. "It's Alan."

"Well," Kieran turned to Helgar with a fake smile. She almost laughed since she knew how much effort it took him to manage *that* smile. "This is my girlfriend, Helgar."

"Gentlemen," she smiled and downed the last of her drink. She turned to Kieran then and stood on tiptoes to kiss him. "Would you dance with me, Superman?"

"Anytime... Miss Lane."

This time Alan was the one staring at them as though they each had a satellite stapled to their heads. Leaving him to ponder, Helgar and Kieran took to the floor: the journalist and her superhero.

Alan shifted his weight from one foot to the other. It was close to midnight since the muted programme around the club aired soft porn as a backdrop. It was clearly making Alan uncomfortable. They were just finishing the last of their drinks when Dylan finally made an appearance. "*Hola fellas!*" he said patting them each on the back. He stepped away from them and held his hand out for a beautiful young woman who had stepped up closer.

"I want you to meet my fiancée, Dianna Jeppe."

Dianna wasn't very tall. Her dark blonde hair was a sleek flowing mass of silk as it steamed down the back of her short purple cocktail dress. She shook hands with Alan as Dylan introduced them; then she took Wesley's. She broke out in a curious smile. "We meet again Wesley Johnson!"

Wesley smiled back at her after hesitating, "Yes. You're Kristen's friend."

"That I am."

Dylan looked between Dianna and Wesley. He touched a hand to his chest in mock despair. No matter what, he trusted Dianna. She was perfection incarnate in every way possible.

She slapped him with her purse. "Don't be silly, Dylan. We met on closing night after the show.

"Wesley and Kris had drinks and he was kind enough to give her a ride home."

Dylan raised his drink at Wesley. "Kris is a fox! You must see her do cabaret."

"A fox?" Wesley chuckled. If only his friend knew how very foxy she really was. His heart skipped a beat suddenly. Just the thought of Kristen sent blood rushing to his groin. He gestured between Dylan and Dianna. "How long are the two of you dating? And, how did you meet?"

Dianna took the liberty of answering, "We met in Feb. I was on my way to meet Kristen for a run one Friday morning. She called to say that the gardens were barricaded due to the opening of Parliament, but I was already on the corner of Wale and Adderley.

"Then I tripped over those silver thingies that looks like that stuff athletes jump over when they –"

Dylan interrupted, "Speed fences."

"Yeah," Dianna winked at him. "Speed fences. And, before I hit the ground, Dylan caught me."

"She literally fell for me," he took a sip of his beer.

"I did. I fell head over heels."

"We've been having coffee everyday since then. Sundays we just spend the entire day together." Dylan winked at his friend.

"That explains a heck of a lot. Wale Street?" Wesley raised his brows at Dylan.

"The law school in Adderley is so to say on the corner right next to the bank," Dylan said more seriously. And, with a loud crash, Dylan and Wesley turned to where shattered glass sounded to one side.

"Crap," Alan shrugged. "Someone's bleeding. It's time for the good doctor to have a look." He walked up to the loud girls lounging about in their very short, very sexy dresses.

Dylan and Wesley exchanged astonished glances.

"What is it?" Dianna asked, picking up on the silent question.

Dylan pointed at the group where Alan was tending to a girl of Japanese slenderness. "See that? That is Alan in doctor mode. That is the only time that Alan can be around beautiful women without ejaculating."

Dianna rolled her eyes at him. "Get real!"

"It's true," Wesley turned back to her. "Alan doesn't have the balls to pickup a girl."

"We find it strange when he is in doctor mode. See, in doctor mode, Alan gets all the hot chicks."

The night seemed to go by quickly. Wesley pushed his way through the crowded floor with the last round of drinks in his hands. He joined the trio who was now talking to the girl who had been cut on the hand by broken glass.

She was thinner and taller close up. The turquoise and black snake-print dress hugged her body. The boobtube dress could easily pass as a skirt if she pulled it lower, and even then it would be too short even to be called that. Despite hanging on Alan's arm, she was looking Wesley up and down. It was so obvious that her attention had shifted to him.

Dylan broke the tension, "Wesley, meet Alan's latest patient, Hailey Langenhoven. Hailey is a first year law student."

Wesley shook hands with the girl who made no secret of the fact that she wanted to get to know him better. "First year law, huh?"

"Yes," her voice was a deep murmur. "I decided law would be a good career considering the fact that I have this pressing sexual fantasy of having the wildest, most passionate sex in the witness box."

Wesley didn't flinch. He simply smiled at her politely, "That's an original one."

Dylan noticed the deep red shade that Alan had gone, and swiftly steered the conversation to cut Hailey out completely. "I never would have thought that Kris would fall for a guy like you."

Wesley shrugged, "I'm just as shocked."

"Kris?" Hailey grimaced. "Are you gay?" She gaped at Wesley. "Not that there is anything wrong with being gay these days," Hailey added a bit too hastily to make the statement plausible.

Dianna's eyes went wide with mock innocence, "Oh yes, as gay as they come, aren't you Wesley?" It wasn't a lie, of course. Dianna had meant gay, as in happy, not as in homosexual.

Wesley nodded.

Alan raised questioning eyebrows at Dylan, "Kris?" He thought for a few seconds, then as though he'd been struck by lightening he said, "Oh yes. Kris!" he touched his head. "My mind is elsewhere."

Dylan's gaze lingered over Hailey's bust, "I would be worried too."

Dianna bowed her head to hide her amusement; Wesley turned his attention over his shoulder to watch the commercial break with a comical smirk, and Alan steered Hailey toward the dance floor to save her and himself further embarrassment.

Percival Van Sitter's guards slowly circled the couple kissing on the dance floor. He had identified the tall male as a police officer. One of his boys had warned him on his arrival that Kieran Clarke was at the club, but he did promise Lutzio Montello that he'd show him the market for their products. Percival was a house name in clubs across Cape Town. He had a few of his own establishments in the northern suburbs, and despite his active drug relations in the most popular clubs in Cape Town, management of the establishments were oblivious to his dark dealings right under their noses. Percival was a professional at pulling a blindfold over their eyes with his local entertainment contacts. If a club was in need of a performer at the last minute or a live band that could imitate the best international acts, Percival delivered at a reasonable price. If they needed five thousand people to attend a certain event, Percival ensured that seven thousand people attended. Whether it was a surplus of imported liquor or cigarettes below cost price, Percival was the man who made it all happen. In return, he was at the top of all guest lists and constantly networking with management. And, of course like tonight, given access to the back luxurious suites where he could do business with his international contacts like the Italian businessman Lutzio Montello.

Their plan was falling into place and running along according to schedule. The premier's office had couriered letters and permits for the lab in Hawston. Percival did however notice his new partner's distractedness, but wisely decided against prying.

It was the part of the night Helgar hated the most. The jazz songs were becoming slower and before she knew it, Kieran was sweeping her in his arms and two-stepping. It wasn't as though they were really there on a date. She just happened to get a tip off from a reliable source that there were some undercover pushers dealing outside and around the club. There were rumours going about of a new social drug that was a combination of cocaine and marijuana, but in the form of a colourful-coated pill. The nifty little thing seemed to be popular among youngsters, especially students, and leave it to Helgar, the bionic journo to blow that shit wide open. The fact that it was her off night meant nothing. A quick peek at Kieran's mobile messages was the perfect front. She knew him too well. Despite their 'date', he was scanning the room with his eagle eyes. It wasn't the usual fleeting scan. It was that trained deliberate lingering scan that he did under his lashes. She pulled away from him slightly. He was doing it now.

"What?" He asked suddenly aware of her staring at him.

"This dance would mean so much more if you could just switch off."

He still didn't look at her when he spoke. "It's second nature. I can't just turn it off."

Helgar sighed. "For once, just forget I'm a journalist and tell me what's going on. If it's that new drug *Gems* you're on about, I know all about it. Please Kieran. Talk to me like I'm your girlfriend."

He shook his head slightly, "That's even more reason not to tell you. It is so dangerous even dancing with you like this. You never know who could be watching."

Helgar sighed, and drew him closer to her until her mouth was an inch from his ear, "Talk to me."

"It's drugs yes. But we also have a lead to the guy who is supposedly distributing it in clubs."

She burned to ask whether she could get the exclusive, but decided that if she was going to crack this story, Kieran could and would under no circumstances be her source.

"It's a foreigner. All we know is that he is Italian. It's believed that his daughter owns some or other sports pub in Greenpoint. We've been watching the place for a while. It seems that the manager is a local woman. None of the staff seems to have met the owner. So that's a mystery to us. All we know about the owner is that she is an Italian national that has applied for citizenship. No one seems to know where this woman is."

"I could find out for you."

"No thank you. I don't want you involved in any of this. Turns out that our guy was at the sports bar with a local merchant, and wait for it – the premier."

"Wilhelmina Langenhoven?"

Kieran nodded, "Too weird?"

"What were they discussing?"

"We couldn't get in that close. We do have a list of everyone who worked on that particular day, but one. There is a young woman who shows up every now and again. She is not on a payroll - so I'm guessing a cash cheque. But, she is a student, so I doubt she's the mob princess Montello."

There it was. More information than she had hoped for. Helgar was trained well enough to know that she should under no circumstances make him aware of his slip up. She listened as he talked briefly about his men trying to get hold of the premier's office after the extended lunch.

"Sure you don't want my help?" she offered one last time."

Kieran took hold of her shoulders before searching her bright green eyes. "No poppet. I just want you to be safe."

She wanted to shake him and tell him that she wanted him safe too, but instead, allowed him to kiss her in the middle of the crowded dance floor.

### Wale Street, CBD, Cape Town
### Friday, 20 March 2008
### 00h10am

Someone had been in her apartment, or worse – still was. Kristen stood in the doorway with her guitar and handbag slung over one shoulder, and her key in her hand. She could tell by the way her cushions were arranged, and by the ruffled rug that separated the foyer from the lounge. But most importantly, her alarm didn't go off. Her skin crawled all over. At that moment her female instinct kicked in as she glanced around the apartment to make sure there was no one within striking distance. The constriction of breath made her ears zing as she slowly backed out the door.

She knew it wasn't Wesley. Dianna had sent her a text just a few minutes before she left the theatre. He was still very much clubbing with his friends.

A loud thump from the balcony sent her bolting into the communal passage. She stumbled away from the danger that lurked on the other side of her sliding door. Her weight seemed to pull her down. The lift seemed so far away and she knew there was no way that she could face the stairwell in her condition, unless a broken neck was on the cards.

"Come on. Come on," she prayed, jabbing the down button of the lift. Just a quick ride in the lift and she could alert security. The metallic grinding of the lift made her oxygen-deprived body sway as it came to a halt. Relief for the salvation that was seconds away made it almost impossible to suppress the quivering sigh that escaped her. In one fluid motion, the doors slid open and her relief was soon replaced with fear.

The man whose black eyes bored into her made her stumble backwards. It was the man who she spent most of her life running away from. The man who had guaranteed her that there was nowhere on earth she could run without him finding her.

And, for a long time, Kristen had believed that she was free of her demons.

This moment proved her wrong.

Lutzio Montello was moving in on her with the same deliberate slowness of a cobra before striking.

"Kristina," his deep accented voice was low and quiet, though hostility peppered the surface.

"Papa…" she gasped airily, unable to move.

His gaze froze her.

This was not happening.

There was no way that he could have tracked her down.

It was now or never. She had to get away. Kristen spun around on her heels and made a hasty, but clumsy run for the dimly lit stairwell.

Panic, tears and resentment was so intense within her that her vision became blurry for a few seconds. She heard Lutzio's heavy labored footsteps as he treaded behind her.

Kristen knew her father too well to know that Lutzio Montello wouldn't call her name, as the echo would alert possible dwellers in adjacent hallways. She was also faster and more agile than the old man who was clearly not going to give up.

She could see the landing between the first and ground floors. The wind from basement stole up the stairs. It would be the perfect get away if she could get to her car, but opening the doors and waiting for the boom to open would take up so much time and Lutzio would catch up with her. If she got to the ground floor, she could cut across the reception area and bolt out the Church Street exit and sprint all the way up to Long Street. Disappearing in Long Street was easy enough with all the clubs and bars open until late.

The door at the entrance to the ground floor lobby slammed shut in front of her, sending her slamming into the rock hard masculine body of a tall dark stranger.

Kristen felt her heart in her throat, muting her cries.

Lutzio's pace slackened behind them and he panted heavily.

Her body went limp in defeat.

Kristen rolled her head back to seek the identity of her captor. The familiar sneer and eyes identical to hers made her stomach reel.

"Sorella," came the thick Italian accent of Vito Goliath Montello. "How nice of you to invite us to catch up on old times."

Kristen wriggled and twisted to escape him, but a well-timed slap through her mouth sent her slamming to the ground.

### Strandfontein, Mitchell's Plain, Cape Town
### Friday, 21 March 2008
### 01h45am

There was no way Dylan was going to drive all the way to Mowbray to drop Dianna, and drive to the city and then drive all the way to Strandfontein alone. It was a good thing Wesley carried the keys to his parents' house. By the time they'd gotten close to Strandfontein on the N7, Dylan turned to Wesley. How's your head?"

"Good. It's throbbing a bit right now after being in the club and having some beer."

"Some beer?" Dylan mocked as he gave his friend a sidelong glance. "You had 3 bottles of beer - 350ml to be exact. Don't be telling me the beer gave you a headache."

Wesley touched a subconscious hand to his head. "You obviously never had a concussion before." He rolled his head slowly to try and ease the tension in his shoulders.

Dylan sent him a sidelong glance. "So you and Kristen are together?"

"Yes. And, man, she is so different from the rest."

Dylan nodded, "I know what you mean. I've met her a few times. She doesn't talk much. She's from England, right?

"Italy. She grew up between Milan and Rome."

Dylan cooed. "Nice. I bet she is the daughter of some really rich Italian politician."

"Try entrepreneur."

"Even better. Though, you seem rather at ease with all of that info. I mean… you tend to be so stiff around rich people."

Wesley snorted. "That's only the construction industry, because the local construction companies are dominated by *verkrampte* whites."

"Not all whites are bigots my friend."

"I know that. Not all coloureds are gangsters."

"I sometimes wonder if this country will ever move away from stereotypes." Dylan drove onto the curb and parked half in the street and half on the pavement. He cut the engine and rested his head against the headrest. "It's a cool thing what you've done for your folks, Wes. I'm thinking of sending my dad and his girlfriend to Knysna for a week. It'll do them good. They're having relationship problems," Dylan snorted. "More like commitment issues from my dad's side if you ask me."

"One problem you certainly didn't inherit from him."

Dylan shook his head. "No. Dianna is the one. I feel it. She is definitely my soul mate."

Wesley gave his friend a fond punch on the shoulder. "Yeah man. I'm happy for you. She's really great." He undid the seatbelt and opened the car. "You're picking me up tomorrow right?"

"Yeah. Before 8am though. I'm taking Dianna to Good Friday mass."

Wesley's brows shot up to his hairline in surprise. "You're going to sit through three hours of meditation and prayer?"

Dylan sighed and gave a timid smile. "I guess so…"

"Okay. She's definitely the one!" Wesley slammed the door shut and jogged up to the front door where he let himself in and flashed the outside light twice to signal that he was okay. He heard Dylan's car roar to life and drive off smoothly.

After his shower and change of clothes, Wesley went into the kitchen. The only thing he craved after a night clubbing was orange juice.

The entire house was dark except the light from the TV in a backroom that doubled as a TV room and a study. Wesley reached into the refrigerator for the litre of orange juice when the telephone in the lounge rang. He shut the door without taking the juice out, and went to answer the telephone. "Johnson." For a few seconds all he heard was wind on the other end, then there was a hissing sound as though someone was running and trying to catch his or her breath.

"Hello?" Wesley asked.

"Wesley? Is that you?" The man's voice was a crackling hiss.

Alarm bells went off in his already throbbing head.

Everyone he knew *knew* that he no longer lived with his parents. At this point, only Dylan knew that he was there. Not even Alan or Kristen knew where he was. He knew that it wasn't Dylan. "Yes. Who is this?"

"Open a door for me *broer*!" the voice sounded choked. "They're going to find me! Oh God!"

There were gunshots.

Wesley froze.

It was so loud, it sounded as though it came from inside the house.

Wesley crawled into the lounge where he ducked beside a window with the wall as a shield. "Who is this?"

"It's me! It's Jacques! Open the door! They're going to find me."

"Who is going to find you?" Wesley rose to his feet slowly and peeked out of the window through the curtains. The front yard was lit up like a soccer stadium at night. When he flicked the lights to signal Dylan earlier, he must have left it on instead of off. And, he didn't check it again. "Where are you Jacques? I'm looking through the curtain." A movement on the ground against the low fence grabbed his attention. He hardly recognised the man that lay there crumpled in a ball.

Dark blood was smeared on the inside wall of the fence.

"Shit, Wesley... They got me good." He made a gurgling sound like someone who was snoring.

There was movement across the street and a gang of five armed men dressed in long eerie black leather coats came closer to the fence. Wesley felt the blood drain from his body as he watched the bloody scene play out in front of him. "Jacques... lay still..." he managed to choke out.

The noise from outside and the wind howling on the phone and under the door made it impossible to hear what Jacques was whispering. His mind was racing. What the hell was Jacques doing at his parents' house? He couldn't remember ever telling any of his colleagues that he was raised in Strandfontein, or even that he lived in the city. What was going on?

It seemed that the neon blue light of Jacques's cellphone was the bull's eye that led the men to the fence.

A thousand words ran through Wesley's mind and he strained to hear what the men were saying to Jacques before one spat down at him before shooting the cellphone from his hand. More shots rang out, this time making Jacques's entire body jerk with the force of it.

And, as though his thoughts were screaming, a stray bullet shattered the window and hit his diploma off the wall on the far side of the lounge, missing his head by millimeters.

Wesley fell to the ground instinctively.

He lay low for a few seconds while dialing 10111.

There were scuffling noises at the garden gate, but he refused to let himself peek.

He called Dylan next.

It felt like an eternity had gone by before he heard sirens. He pressed himself up against the wall and peeked through the curtains.

Jacques's body was gone.

The only evidence of the gory memory was the thick dark blood splatter against the white fence.

### *College Road,* Athlone, Cape Town
### *Friday, 21 March 2008*
### *02h20am*

Thank the heavens for small mercies; Helgar thought the moment the police radio crackled. The absence of a car lighter in her little Fiat had been a nightmare for the past four months. She was in the Little Karoo on a story when her cellphone's battery died. In her haste to purchase a car charger, she'd thrown the damn lighter out with the packaging. Right now she realised it was a blessing in disguise. Kieran had walked her to the parking lot when she couldn't find her funky little pocket lighter in her bag, he steered her toward the unbranded police car a few rows down. He pulled the door open for her, and walked over to his colleague who was crossing the lot toward them.

Helgar grabbed her tiny notebook from her purse and scribbled down the address that was broadcast over the small police radio.

"All available units," the woman's calm voice reminded her of announcements on metro stations. "We have a shooting out in Strandfontein, close to the Spar right off Baden Powell."

The address followed and Helgar prayed that she'd manage to conceal her notebook before Kieran got back. She lit a cigarette and got out of the car with a perfect neutral face.

She smiled at him when he took her into his arms. "So," she stood on the tips of her toes and gave him a lingering kiss. Pretenses came naturally to her, though it took extra concentration around Kieran. "Are you coming over to my place or do I have to follow you to yours?"

He buried his face in her hair. "Hmm… Why don't we go to my place? You can lead the way."

"And what are we going to do there?" she asked seductively.

"Everything," he whispered into her ear. The next moment his cellular phone vibrated in his shirt's pocket. He kissed her quickly on the lips before checking the number, "It's the office."

Helgar nodded for him to take the call while she turned slightly so that she could view the entrance of the club. By the time she finished her smoke Kieran was at her side. "Poppet…"

"You have to leave?" she asked - disappointment heavy in that rhetorical question.

He nodded. "Will you be okay to get to your car?"

"Yes Kieran. You go do your job..."

He smiled and winked at her before getting into the white sedan.

Helgar watched him back out of the parking lot, "...and I'll do mine." She reached into her bag again, and whipped out her cellphone. "It's Helgar. I need a photographer to meet me in Strandfontein." She gave the address and ran over to her car. She opened the trunk, took out a duffle bag and then got into the back where she changed into brown sweats. She leaned forward and emptied a bottle of water over her hair that she found in the bag, and sleeked her hair back where she tied it. A black baseball cap went on her head and black sneakers on her feet. She got out makeup removing pads and wiped her face clear of makeup. With that, she jumped into the driver's seat and stepped on the gas.

She had her excuse all worked out if Kieran recognised her on the crime scene. She'd simply say she was getting ready for bed when she got a call from her editor or a reliable source. Her editor was a safe bet, as she'd meet up with a photographer.

Alan heard screeching wheels for the second time while he lay on the back seat of Hailey's red VW Jetta.

She was stoned.

That was obvious.

Her sex drive was rocketing by the minute as she took him to his peak over and over again. It wasn't like Alan to prey on drugged females, but he was powerless against Hailey and her hot little body. "Hailey... for goodness sake... slow down."

"No!" she threw her head back and took him even deeper inside her. Alan turned slightly. The air was stale in the car. The windows were steamed up. The one moment Hailey was screaming out in pleasure, and the next, she'd passed out cold right on top of him. He needed a girlfriend – a real one - a girl who didn't overdo substances like alcohol and drugs. He re-thought that. "No drugs," he corrected himself. The car gave a sudden jerk. The next moment, he and Hailey both tumbled down the seat. He was now lying on top of her on the floorboard that separated the backseat from the two front seats.

"Shit!" Alan cursed out loud. "We're being towed away!"

Thankfully, Hailey was fully dressed in the clothes he'd met her in. Alan struggled into his pants and his jacket. By the time the tow truck came to a halt, he was dressed and ready to talk to the towing service worker.

It was a young man sporting a nametag that read Sydney.

Sydney had almost jumped straight into the air when Alan tapped him on the shoulder. "Man! You scared me!"

"I'm sorry, man. I just want to know what the deal is. My girlfriend and I fell asleep in the car. She wasn't feeling well and took some pills. I guess we both fell asleep."

"You were parked in a no-parking zone."

"Okay. I just have to pay the fine right? Then we can get the car back?"

Sydney shook his head. "No sir. We have to keep the car for 48 hours. I've already dispatched the plate number."

Alan ran his hands through his hair. "What now? How do I get back to the club with her in this condition?"

Sydney shrugged. "Look… I can give you a ride back, but I can't give you back the car."

Alan nodded. "Okay. Let me just get my girl." He reached into the car and took Hailey into his arms and placed her on the backseat of the yellow 1985 Ford Escort beside the tow truck. He went back to the car to get her handbag. It was lodged under the backside of the passenger seat. He pulled with a little effort and out slipped a manila A4 envelope. The name and address was printed on a sticker:

*The Premier*
*Ms Wilhelmina Langenhoven*

"Hell's bells…" Alan sighed. His head snapped to the yellow car a few feet away. "Hailey Langenhoven…" He read enough about her in the local tabloids, but now Hailey Langenhoven had chosen him as her one nightstand. Alan wanted to strangle her as he stomped back to the yellow car. *She* was Hailey Langenhoven! Sydney was already driving when Alan flipped the back flap of the envelope and peeped at the contents. It looked like blueprints, some press releases, photographs and bonds for a location in Hawston. He started pulling the first page free when his cellphone rang.

It was Dylan calling. "Hey man!"

"Alan, you have to come by the Johnson's house. I have bad news. There was a shooting incident."

"What? Is Wesley okay? Has he been hit?"

Dylan's voice was shaky on the other end. "He hasn't been wounded, but he's going to need a shot. The paramedics are tending to three people who got injured."

"I'll be right there." Alan turned to Sydney. "How fast can you get this piece of shit to the club?"

Sydney frowned at him. "We're here man. Don't bite the hand."

He pulled Hailey from the car and placed her on the back seat of his car together with the envelope. A tap on his window sounded. It was two of Hailey's friends we'd recognised from the club and still dressed in outfits similar to Hailey's.

"Thank God! Her car was impounded. We went over to the yard, but they refused to let me pay the fine. She fell asleep. Can you guys see her safely home?"


## Strandfontein, Cape Town
### Friday, 21 March 2008
### 03h40am

Yellow and blue police tape cordoned off the house from the crowd that gathered outside the Johnson house. It was close to 4am. Christians would soon be making their way to church for the first mass of the Good Friday. Helgar heard from the stirring crowd that someone was shot in the inside of the property. No one was sure if the owner had shot anyone, or if the owner had found the gunman. Some said it was a drive-by shooting and a bullet went through the front window of the house they all staked out. The place was crawling with cops. Helgar made her way to the far side of the crowd where police vehicles stood abandoned. A young officer stood scribbling on a clipboard. She rubbed her eyes until they stung and faked a sob. She walked over to the officer. "Oh thank God!" she said spirited. "Is he in there? Is he okay? They won't let me in!" she clung to him hysterically. "Is he hurt?"

The young constable gave her a sympathetic smile. "Are you a relative?"

"Yes," her voice crackled. She wiped her tearing eyes. "What happened?"

The constable hesitated for a second. Then he looked at the woman in front of him. She was clearly distraught. "Wesley is alright, ma'am," he said. "At this time it just looks like a stray bullet took out that window," he pointed to the large shattered window in the front of the house facing the road, "and missed him by inches."

Helgar slapped a hand over her mouth and shook her head for extra dramatics. "You have any suspects yet officer?"

"Not at this time."

"If it wasn't Wesley who was shot, *who* was shot?"

"That we don't know ma'am. There was no body, which means the victim got away. We have men checking the hospitals and health centres right now."

Helgar nodded. "Thank you. Did he see anything?"

"He is being questioned as we speak. Please stick around though. He's going to need the support."

She smiled dryly, "Of course." She backed away from the officer when she saw Kieran approaching. Ducked behind a police car, she could hear him.

"Saunders? Did you alert the medical centres?"

"Yes Captain. The crime scene manager found this near the gate."

Helgar lifted her head slightly to see what the constable was showing Kieran. It looked like a silver cap of a pen that was placed in a zip lock bag.

"Bullet shells?"

"That is not all, sir. There is an inscription on the side of it. Looks like some fancy engraving."

Helgar took out her notebook and scribbled. There was a familiar voice that made her curious. She ducked behind the car and strode back to the crowd. She followed the sound of the voice. It was the three men from the club. Dylan, Alan and - oh sweet heaven – Wesley Johnson.

## Shortmarket Street, CBD, Cape Town
### Friday, 21 March 2008
### 05h50am

The lack of sleep together with his concussion and the night he'd had made Wesley grumpy. Alan had given him a shot to calm him down, but he was still anxious by the time Dylan had driven him home. Alan sat beside him in the back seat.

"This is seriously messed up," Alan ran a hand over his face. "It's almost freaky."

"Creepy is more like it," Dylan said from the front seat. "How did that guy know you'd be at your parents' place? And, never mind that. How did he get hold of the telephone number? Your dad's not listed."

Wesley shrugged. "I'm just glad that you guys weren't there or even Kristen for that matter."

Alan nodded in agreement. "Hell Wesley. You were almost shot."

"I know. Rather me than someone else."

"Rather your scaly colleague than you," Dylan said while watching his friends in the rearview mirror. He pulled into the small parking bay outside Wesley's flat.

Alan opened stretched as he got out of the car. "We could all do with some sleep."

"You guys can crash here for a few hours. I just want to get inside and give Kristen a call." He turned to Dylan. "Did you tell Dianna?"

"No. I figured she'd tell Kristen immediately and I didn't want anyone panicked."

Wesley nodded in thanks. "I could do with coffee and a cigarette."

"We all could," Alan took the keys from Wesley and opened the door to the ground floor flat. He stepped back with his hands out in front of him.

Dylan and Wesley were both on high alert.

"Dylan," Alan said in a low voice, "Call Captain Clarke. I don't think last night was a coincidence."

Wesley pushed past Alan and froze in the doorway of his bachelor pad. "What the fuck?"

His entire flat was turned upside down.

"Don't touch anything!" Dylan shouted from behind him. "Clarke said he'd be here in ten minutes." His words were barely spoken when his cellphone rang again. He held it out to Wesley. "You need to get your cell replaced man. I feel like a damn PA."

Alan poked Dylan in the back. "Bad joke man."

Wesley took the phone. "Wesley."

"Wesley, I know this is going to sound strange, but please don't mention my name," sounded the deep female voice on the other end.

"Okay. I'm listening."

"We met last night at the club. I was with Kieran Clarke. Do you remember me?"

"I do," Wesley confirmed.

"I understand that you know the man who was shot. I just want to know if you think it's drug-related."

"Excuse me?"

"Please don't hang up. Can we meet? I can't talk about this over the phone, but I have reason to believe that an Italian mafia family is behind this. Whatever happened last night at your house in Strandfontein involved the mafia."

Wesley let out a long hard sigh. "Isn't that just a little too crazy?"

"No not at all. Especially since the family in question have already started making in roads here in Cape Town. It seems that the man you saw get shot, Jacques Cloete, was on a hit list for evading street taxes on drugs. I have in my possession a bullet shell from last night, and it turns out that the same marking on it belongs to a notorious Italian narcotics kingpin by the surname Montello. Police believe that his daughter owns a little pub in Greenpoint called the Krimson Kimono."

"Oh my God… Are you serious?"

"As a heart attack, yes. When can we meet?"

"Tuesday."

"There is a little coffee shop on Greenmarket Square. It's called *Familia Amelia*. I'll wait for you at the last table at the far side of the bar. After 5pm?"

"Yes. That's fine. Thanks again for the call." Wesley turned off the phone and handed it back to Dylan who was now talking to Captain Clarke and his sidekick.

After a thorough comb of the flat, Kieran appeared in the doorway where he concentrated his weight to his arm propped against the doorframe. He fixed his neon blue eyes on Wesley. "Mr Johnson," he pulled a tiny little zip lock bag from the breast pocket of his black flak jacket and held it up to his temple. It contained a silver bullet shell identical to the ones found at his parents' house earlier that morning. "Are you sure there is nothing that you want to tell me?"

Alan and Dylan exchanged surprised looks.

Wesley shook his head. "That's not mine. I haven't been here since I got my head bashed at work the day of the blackout."

"That's not what I mean," Kieran searched the younger man's face. "The lock of a cupboard in your bedroom was shot to hell. Someone is looking for something that they think you have Mr. Johnson. Do you have any idea what that can be?"

"No. I don't have anything valuable here. The locked cupboard in my bedroom just has all my sports equipment, electronic keyboard and some clothes I've boxed and marked for charity."

Kieran nodded thoughtfully. "Then everything is still there." The vibration from a second breast pocket sent his hand instinctively patting the front of the heavy protective jacket. "Clarke," he said into the phone.

Wesley turned back to his friends. "What the hell is going on guys? What could anyone possibly want from me?"

"We're here for you, Wes. Doesn't matter what anyone does or says. We're your friends, and you have us," Alan said.

"I've called Dianna. I'll meet up with her after mass," Dylan shrugged. "You should probably let Kristen know what's going on."

Kieran appeared once again. "Do you have somewhere you can stay until we get a team out here to dust for fingerprints?"

Wesley nodded. "I'm just going to need some clothes." He turned back to Dylan. "Would you call Kristen and ask her if it's okay for me to stay with her? I won't be long." Wesley and Kieran went into the flat, emerging a few minutes later with a trolley suitcase and a tog bag.

Dylan took the trolley from him. "Kristen's at the Krimson Kimono. She said she's checking the geysers. The place is apparently closed today."

"Can you drive me over there?"

Dylan nodded.

Kieran cleared his throat. "What is she doing there if they're closed?"

Wesley shrugged. "She helps out whenever the boss needs her." Immediately, he regretted offering that information. "At least that's what the manager once told me."

"Really?" Kieran raised a brow before righting himself. "Gentlemen," he spoke in a suddenly cheerful voice. "I bid you a fair day. Wesley, get some rest."

Alan gave the police captain a mock hand salute and followed Dylan and Wesley to their cars. "Are you okay to drive Johnson?" Alan asked.

"I'm fine. I have to get to Kristen." Wesley was already sitting behind the wheel of his car. "I'll call you guys later. Thanks for last night."

Dylan and Alan nodded in unison as Wesley drove off.


## Krimson Kimono, Greenpoint, Cape Town
*Frida, 21 March 2008*
*07h50am*

Kristen was just about finished with the security checks of the Krimson Kimono when her cellphone rang. She hadn't recognised the number, therefore hesitating before she answered.

It wasn't her father, neither her brother.

She let out a deep breath.

Instead, it was Dylan, Dianna's dish of a boyfriend. At first she was confused as to why Dylan would be calling her about Wesley, and then, it all became clear to her. Dylan was one of the guys she'd seen Wesley with the night when Torea performed.

Small world.

Though Dylan wasn't clear about the problem, he was clear about Wesley needing somewhere to stay until "it" was sorted out. It was the "it" she didn't quite get, but she was more than ecstatic to have Wesley stay for a few more days – that was, knowing Lutzio and Vito were only returning on Tuesday. They mentioned to her, after shoving her around and giving her a lecture; that they would be in a small fishing town until then. She'd missed the name they'd said. She was too busy concentrating on mending her bumps and bruises on her body that would make people stare and ask questions - especially Wesley. Her brother was the brawn – that was for sure. Vito always had a way of leaving marks on her body that would and could be covered with simple clothing. She had long since learnt that the only way to make him stop was not to fight against him as it only fueled his rage. She also perfected masking her fear of him over the years. Last night was different.

Last night, it was the fear that they might learn about her love affair with Wesley that had her singeing with it. And, even more so, the fear that Wesley might have walked in on that unsightly scene in her apartment. If either Vito or her father knew about Wesley, neither of them had said anything.

Kristen crossed her hands over her chest. She caught a glimpse of the purple-red bruise on her forearm. The ointment the pharmacist swore by years ago to speed up the healing process was working miracles indeed. The zinc oxide content was high enough to make the bruise appear less fresh.

The slamming of the door behind her made her jump. Her heart was in her throat.

And then she saw him slumped against the door. The only man who had shown her that love and tenderness could exist in harmony.

"Wesley…" she breathed his name, propelling herself at him. Then she stopped. Gasping in fright she asked, "What happened to you?"

He shook his head rapidly. "I was caught in the middle of something ugly. I witnessed a murder. I was shot at and whoever done it knows where I live."

Kristen took a step back. She looked outright horrified. "Are you alright? Were you shot?"

Wesley shook his head again. "No." His mind was suddenly clear when he looked into her big frightened green shadowed eyes. The sound of her choked cries gutted him. Pulling her into the secure circle of his arms, he kissed her soft cascading locks. "I took a blow to the head, but I'm okay."

Kristen drew in a deep breath. She wanted to drown in his scent. The heat of his body stole through the thin T-shirt she wore. The feel of his rapid but strong heartbeat against her cheek was proof that she could never have felt that glorious pounding if a bullet had ripped through it.

She sniffed.

And then she went into an uncontrollable fit of crying.

"Hey," Wesley pulled her away from him gently. "What's wrong?"

His heart skipped a beat.

There was some swelling to the side of her cheek. The back of his hand touched the angry redness of it. Frowning, he held her gaze. "What happened?"

"I slipped," she lied.

His hand fell away from her face. Lowered brows sent shadows swimming in his dark eyes.

"I was in the bathroom. I missed the mat and slid across the floor." She crossed her arms over her chest and walked over to the platform that served as a stage. It's where she'd left the keys to the place and her handbag.

"You'd have to think up something better to tell me Kristen. You don't just hurt your face when you slip on wet tiles."

She froze.

It felt as though his eyes bore right through her. "I didn't just hurt my face. My whole body took the punch."

Literally.

Now that wasn't a lie, she thought. That was the honest truth. She turned around to look him in the eyes. What she saw there was genuine concern.

He crossed the floor to her in three quick strides. Lifting her into his arm, he held her. Her heart pounded against his chest. "I'm sorry," he whispered in her hair. "I should have been there."

Kristen's mind flooded with multiple scenarios if Wesley had been with her, let alone in her apartment when Vito arrived.

She shuddered at the thought. "No. I'm just sorry that I didn't finish in time to meet you at the club. Freda gave me a ride back. We got held up by the director of some new local television series."

The way her body melted with his the way it had just now made Wesley's blood soar.

The sound of her voice cut into his thoughts. He placed her on her feet. "I'm sorry. I didn't hear a word you said."

She walked over to her handbag and pulled out two shiny keys dangling from a silver dog tag key-chain. "It's for you," she held it out to him. "I had it made for you."

The way colour crept into her face when she blushed made him dizzy with adoration.

"Dylan said you needed a place to stay for a few days."

Wesley walked up to her. He took the keys from her. It jingled in his palm when he moved it.

At some point, the sun had disappeared behind a thick layer of dark gray clouds.

It began to rain.

"How did you get here?" she asked, lifting her head once more.

Wesley curled his fingers over the keys. "I drove."

"What is it?" Kristen asked when he grunted.

He was already halfway to the door. "I didn't lock the car."

"Wesley! You don't have on a coat!" Her words fell on deaf ears. Wesley was already crossing the street.

The wind had picked up and the rain fell harder.

Wesley looked up into the sky. The rain felt good after the past 24 hours he'd had. It had been a long time since he stopped and appreciated its beauty and healing properties.

"Wesley!"

The voice from the doorway of the Krimson Kimono was a reminder to him that there were things in life that were simple miracles. Kristen was one of them.

A look of pure amusement spread across Kristen's face.

Wesley couldn't stop himself from constantly being consumed by her. The walk back into the Krimson Kimono was a slow, intense one. He was soaked with rain, but she didn't budge or shriek out of his embrace.

The moment he planted his hands on her hips, her arms curled around his neck. It felt like a natural response. Wesley was careful in touching her. She had told him that she'd hurt her entire body during the accident she'd had in her bathroom. His fingers threaded through her hair. He touched her face. His knuckles brushed over her arms that were still coiled around his neck. Eventually, he settled his hands below her bottom, lifting her ever so gently, kissed her.

Kristen felt herself soaring.

Heat flushed through her with a torrent of emotions that made her giddy with desire.

She felt his hands on her skin as he sought out every sensitive inch, yet taking great care to soothe the angry bumps on her delicate skin.

She gasped at the plonking and plinking sounds of the piano keys when he'd deposited her on the cold ivory smoothness of them.

He hesitated for a second when he tugged the thin gauzy white T-shirt over her head. Dark purple-black bruises stood out brutally against the natural blushed porcelain of her skin. Smaller greenish-blue marks that seemed to look like marks from a rod of fingers wrapped around one of the balls of her shoulders.

Kristen risked looking at him from under her lashes. "It looks worse than it feels."

His hands cupped her face.

It dawned on him that her injuries could have been a lot worse if she'd been with him at the club. For whatever reason, they could have been trapped outside his parents' house when the gunfight started.

If she'd gotten bruised up this badly from a slide across that bathroom floor, he didn't want to think what could have happened if she'd showed up last night. His forehead touched hers. His voice was a whisper. "I love you, Kitty Cat. You got hurt last night and I wasn't there to help you."

She rubbed her nose against the side of his. "I was clumsy." It was the truth. She should have chosen a different means of escape from her brother and her father. "I should have been more careful," she mumbled.

"I'm just happy that you didn't break anything."

"Just a few bruises. Nothing that won't heal in a few days. Please don't let it bother you."

How could he not be bothered? It looked painful and lumpy at places were the swelling had not yet subsided. His lips moved slowly over one of her bruised shoulders repeatedly as though he were trying to kiss the horrendous discoloration away.

She leaned forward. The movement sent her wet hair brushing the side of his face, making his entire frame stiffen. He tilted her chin with a crooked finger so that he was looking directly into her eyes.

The only sound was the wind slamming rain against the windows and the door. The echo from where the torrent pounded on the raw upper floor roof drowned out the tinker of the piano keys as he adjusted her position to remove her faded blue jeans.

Though her face was bear of makeup, it held a deep apricot radiance to it. Her half-closed eyes sparkled like fairy dust and the full sensual lips, slightly parted sent all his blood rushing to his groin.

Her gaze never left his in all the time that she'd undone his drenched jeans and pushed it down his hips. His skin felt slightly cold where the denim had stuck to his bottom and his thighs. Her hands moved slowly from the expanse of muscle from his lower abdomen, under his shirt, around his exquisitely chiseled back.

Ecstasy broke though his self-control, making his head roll back.

Kristen took full advantage of the exposed throat before her. Her lips latched onto the base of his throat where she teased him with warm lingering kisses, alternatively grazing her teeth over the flesh that now sizzled under her moist tongue.

He couldn't put words to it at that moment, but Kristen Katts was driving him crazy with her sensual teasing. He grunted in frustration, shoving his hands into her damp hair before bringing his mouth down hard on hers. Heat and need combined almost powerful enough to make the air around them crackle. The tangle of arms and legs melded them together in a writhing, passionate act that threatened their balance. He'd be damned if making love to Kristen ended on the floor of the Krimson Kimono. He hoisted her onto the very top of the ebony grand top, only leaving enough time to join her before claiming her mouth again. His fingers dipped into her, teasing and flicking, bringing her close to the edge of madness before he thrust hard and deep into her time and time again. The incoherent sounds that ripped from her throat told him she was almost at her peak. He lifted her hips and thrust even deeper into her where he felt her shatter around him in intense waves of pleasure and contractions that sent him over the edge right behind her. Her soft warmth surrounded him, as they lay spent, panting in each other's arms.

This was heaven - the moment she nuzzled her cheek against his shoulder in breathlessness and still managed to smile up at him. Nothing compared to the weight of his heart when she whispered to him.

"I love you, Wesley Johnson…"

# CHAPTER SIX

*Hout Street, CBD, Cape Town*
*Tuesday, 25 March 2008*
*16h15pm*

Despite the dramatic and unfortunate start of the past Easter weekend, Wesley was a happy man when he returned to work the Tuesday after the family day holiday that wrapped up a blissful few days with Kristen.

A cleaning team approved by SAPS and under their supervision had set to the task of cleaning up Wesley's apartment. During his lunchtime break, he bought some groceries and took a stroll over to his tidy little sitter and was amazed at the accurate job that had been done.

Just before knock off time, Vito Goliath strode into the office with two members of SAPS in tow. The staff huddled together in the middle of the room dragging chairs and stools. Others propped up on the front of their desks.

Vito's dark exotic features grew even darker as he scanned the faces of his staff of 15. "I have bad news."

Wesley shut his eyes. The world seemed to be spinning around him. He locked gazes with Vito, before the boss's eyes drifted to a uniformed officer.

"Our colleague and friend, Jacques Cloete has been murdered. His family has not been informed at this time. The police have asked that we keep this information to ourselves until such time that they do locate his family." The big green eyes of Vito Goliath missed nothing.

Wesley noticed the tiniest movement caught his boss's eye. It was a strange habit, he thought. Immediately after he'd thought it, he felt ashamed that he'd missed the last few sentences before he heard Vito dismiss the team.

## Familia Amelia, Greenmarket Square, CBD, Cape Town
## Tuesday, 25 March 2008
## 16h15pm

Familia Amelia was slightly busier than normal. Helgar pulled out her cellular phone just as the crowd gave way to the dark-eyed man who looked just a little windblown. "Glad you could make it," she said, sliding the mobile device back into her olive utility bag.

Wesley sat down staring in confusion at the massive vase she had been sipping from.

As though reading his thoughts, Helgar gave an amused little chuckle. "It's a *Jam Jar*. The name of the drink, that is. It's got quite a bit of a kick."

Wesley nodded sheepishly. "I'd say. What is that 1.5 litres?"

"Actually, yes." Helgar waved a hand at a waiter who took Wesley's order and returned with a foaming mug of beer.

"I'm going to cut to the chase," Helgar said after a few more sips of her drink. "The guy that was shot and killed at your house is Jacques Cloete. His body was found on Saturday morning just after 8h00 in Hawston."

Wesley ran a hand over his face, "Hawston? What the hell? How do you know all this?"

Helgar rolled her eyes at him. "If I tell you, you have to promise that you'll take it to the grave."

Wesley raised his right hand subconsciously. "Scouts honor."

"I'm dating Clarke. When I called you Saturday, I just had a suspicion. I've picked up a bullet case on the crime scene." She shook her head now, looking at him apologetically. "I went through the police file.

This morning when he was in the shower, I found it in his satchel. I took photographs of the report and printed them when I got to the office.

"The body was found tied to a jetty three meters below the water. According to ballistics reports, the manufacturer of the bullet shells is some exclusive gunsmith in Italy. Interpol is apparently tracking them down as we speak."

Wesley was visibly baffled, "Ballistics? This is South Africa. Don't these things take three years to come back from a lab? It was Easter for Christ's sake!"

Helgar shook her head. "You'd be surprised at the rate Kieran works." She gave a devilish smile, and then she took a deep drink of her Jam Jar. "The blood on the fence was analysed as well. It matches that of the victim. It appears that narcotics experts detected some new substance in the blood. Seems your little friend was drugged heavily that night. Aside from traces of ether, there was cocaine and other substances found in the blood. It is believed that he was killed because he owed thousands to a suspected gangster and drug lord named Percival Van Sitter."

"This doesn't explain why it's taken first priority. People are hunted and killed by drug lords all the time," Wesley drank deeply.

"Right you are, Mr Johnson. Right you are. You see… it turns out that the victim was supplying drugs to university students, who, as you and I both know, are broke most of the time. One of the names on the IOU list found on the victim was none other than Hailey Langenhoven."

Wesley's intense search in his brain had turned up blank. He raised his eyebrows at Helgar, "Who?"

"The Premier's daughter, who so by the way, also happens to be a law student," amusement made her eyes dance for a few seconds before she became serious again. "Your friend Alan, the good doctor, had tended to the injuries of the Princess Langenhoven at the club on Friday night. Ring any bells?"

Wesley fell back in his seat, gaping.

He remembered only too well how that little movie had played itself out.

"Police believe that the new drug ensemble is masterminded by an Italian mafia boss," Helgar went on. "The Italian mafia boss in question is allegedly working with Percival van Sitter. Kieran has been on to him for over a year now. He is just thrown off course when van Sitter keeps proving innocent to dealing in sting ops." She reached into her utility bag once more and handed him the bullet shell. "See the fancy engraving on the case?"

"Yes. Looks like 'M' or something."

"It is. But, you'll also notice the other markings beside it. That is the emblem of the Italian Mafia Boss, Lutzio Montello." She reached under her bag and pulled out a glossy black and white picture sporting a red official SAPS seal in one corner. "This is the bastard," she tapped her finger on the sheet she showed him. A burly, graying man stared out of the photograph. Helgar caught his astonished expression. She smiled at him reassuringly, "Don't worry, Kieran won't miss this one."

Wesley was concerned. "Could he actually arrest you?"

"He has arrested me before. I'm just doing my job."

"So why did you call me?"

Helgar scanned the room as she had every so often since he'd sat down. "You are a suspect."

### *Wale Street, CBD, Cape Town*
### *Wednesday, 26 March 2008*
### *8:45am*

Wednesday morning mass at St George's Cathedral was not what regular attendees had expected. But, as many of the senior citizens lingered, the many pews started filling up with people who attended the memorial service of a young man who had been a whiz kid in the computer business.

Friends and family, close relatives and extended family of the late Jacques Cloete took the pulpit and shared their fondest memories with fellow mourners.

Wesley tried to concentrate, but his mind kept returning to Helgar's words the previous afternoon.

What did it mean that he was a suspect in Jacques murder?

Why - because Jacques was shot in his parents' front yard?

He needed air.

It was a nippy morning, Wesley decided as he fumbled in his pockets for smokes. The thought of even being associated with a murder gave him the creeps. Not even Kristen could take his mind off it. Even while he had made love to her, he kept seeing the splatter of blood on the inside fence in his mind.

Clarke had promised that everything would be restored and cleaned by the time Wesley's parents returned from the North West province.

Wesley strolled through the Company Gardens next to the cathedral. He'd asked Kristen to meet him in the gardens for breakfast, but she wasn't able to due to an audition. Wesley walked over to a *boerewors* roll vendor where he ordered two rolls with relish and tomato sauce and two cups of coffee. He walked over to one of the wooden benches where a homeless man sat adjusting his badly soiled scarf.

"How are you today sir?" Wesley asked the weather-withered man.

The *bergie* stared up at Wesley as though it was the first human conversation he'd had in twenty-five years. "I'm alive, son. God's good graces keep me alive."

Wesley held out a boerewors roll and a hot cup of coffee to the man. "Hungry? I've got an extra meal. My friend can't make it."

The older man graciously accepted the food from Wesley. "Thank you. I haven't had one of these in two years." He bit into the hot sausage, blowing steam and burning his pallet, but the tantalizing aroma of *braaied wors* and the fresh bun won. He spoke while taking a second bite and rolling the delicious food around in his mouth. "My lady and I were evicted from our little place in Woodstock," he said. "I worked at the electrical place there in Salt River," he pointed absent-mindedly in the general direction of the area. "My lady worked at one of the Chinese shops in the main road. Our son was killed in a drive-by shooting one night when he came from a school function." The destitute man sighed heavily. "I went berserk," he shrugged. "Our funeral policy had lapsed because of the school fees we had to pay. I ended up stealing from my employer to finance the funeral. My lady turned to *tik*. I lost my job, she lost hers and we lost the house."

Wesley shrugged. "That's how you ended up here?"

The old man nodded. "Can you believe it?"

"That's life."

"I'm Monray. That," he pointed in the direction of the mountain, "is my lady Bertha."

Wesley saw the slender limping woman approach them wearing a threadbare black tracksuit and a soiled red bandana. The black sneakers on her feet were badly scuffed. Despite the dirt-smeared face, Wesley saw Bertha's friendly face. Under all that grime, he was convinced that she was a very attractive woman. He smiled at her when she came closer to the bench. "Bertha," he nodded. "Monray was just telling me what a busy morning you'd had."

Bertha hardly noticed Wesley, except the food in his hand.

He hadn't touched it yet. He saw where her eyes had settled and held it out to her. "For you," he said handing her the coffee too.

Bertha nodded her thanks and sat down, digging into the roll.

After a few more minutes of light conversation while he smoked, Wesley made his way back to the cathedral.

It wasn't that he saw Vito Goliath crossing the road that made Wesley suspicious. It was the fact that he stared up and settled his gaze on a specific balcony, that got Wesley started up.

His eyes trailed that of Vito's and there was Kristen's balcony door wide open.

The uneasiness that he felt sent warning bells off in his head. Instinctively he followed Vito into the Mandela Rhodes Place.

Wesley's heart dropped into his stomach when he saw Kristen entering the lobby from the St George's Mall entrance. She was talking on her mobile in short furious sentences, barely noticing anyone as she jabbed a finger on the lift's button. "I don't care if it is short notice. Make a plan! Isn't that your job?" she was saying to the person on the other end of the phone.

Wesley noticed something about her voice beside distress. He noticed that a lazy Central European accent had heavily altered her usual British one.

She had slid into the lift, demanding to speak to a manager, almost hysterical.

Quick thinking had Wesley taking an alternate lift up to the third floor. He went up one flight of stairs where he could hear her arguing with a man in a fluent modern Latin tongue, just around the corner from where he stood pressed against the wall and hidden by the shadows of overgrown creepers.

The exchange was angry and high-spirited before a door slammed and the voices were muffled.

After another few minutes of intense bickering, Wesley heard the door open. The male voice had sounded hoarse and gruff when he spoke a short line in the language Wesley didn't understand.

Wesley heard Kristen's breathless voice as well as the sound of her muffled footsteps as she yelled, "Don't you ever come back here again!" It was followed by another fluent rush of the foreign tongue that Wesley could easily interpret as curses.

"Don't count on it, Princess." The accent of the man was familiar. "*Arrividerci!*" he spat.

Now that was a word he understood. And, that one word answered the question of the language.

It was Italian.

The lift slid open.

Wesley moved closer to get a glimpse of the bastard who had just been with his girlfriend. The tremor that ran through his entire being at the sight of Vito Goliath's grim face had set his blood to ice. Some time had gone by before Wesley felt composed enough to confront Kristen.

"Wesley!" the relief was apparent in her voice when she opened the door. "I thought you said you had a memorial service to attend." She flung herself at him. It took her some time to realise that he wasn't holding her, so she unwound herself and stepped back.

Confusion settled over her features. "Are you okay?"

Wesley slumped against the doorframe, arms crossed over his chest. "Who was that?"

Kristen didn't as much as flinch. "Who was who?"

"The man who you were arguing with in fluent Italian. Who was he?"

She shrugged without breaking eye contact. "Someone I used to live with."

"What's going on Kristen?" Wesley asked. His self-control was on the verge of breaking point. "Heated arguments in Italian? Ex lovers –"

"He is not an ex lover!" she retorted, slapping her thighs irritated.

"Then what was Vito Goliath doing here?"

It was the first time she'd heard Wesley raise his voice. She wasn't certain what unnerved her more – the sound of his anger or the fact that he knew her brother's name. "Vito Goliath?" she asked, forgetting to hide her astonishment. She was horrified.

"You heard me. I know who he is."

Alarmed, Kristen backed away. "How do you…?"

"He owns shares in the company I work for."

Again, Kristen gaped.

Her brother owned a legit company in Cape Town?

Could that explain how they'd found her?

How long were they spying on her? Oh no! What if Vito knew about her and Wesley?

"Did he see you?" Kristen's eyes darted over his shoulder.

"I don't think so. And, what if he did?" Wesley challenged.

"Please Wesley, you have to stay away from him," she was close to tears now. "He can never know that you and I are together."

Wesley shook his head in confusion. "What are you hiding from me, Kristen? Tell me," his voice crackled and broke. "Please. If you're seeing someone else–"

"I'm not!" she protested, sinking onto the arm of one sofa. "You are the only one Wesley. Please, you have to believe me. You have to trust me."

His eyes slid from hers to the overstuffed suitcases in the middle of the floor behind her. "When were you going to tell me that you were going somewhere?"

She closed her eyes tightly as she spoke. "Its props and costumes that must be taken back to the Baxter," she opened her eyes again and sighed. "It's such ghastly old cases. Do you really think they're mine? I had it on loan."

She had a point, Wesley thought. Those horrible rotting maroon leather trunks could not belong to Kristen.

He relaxed slightly.

"You're going to have to give me some answers Kristen." He moved to the kitchen where he set the kettle to boil. "That place you're working at. It belongs to some or other mafia boss." He watched the colour drain from her face.

"W-what?" Her nails dug into her palms from the balled fists she realised she'd made. "Who told you that?"

"It's not important. But the police are on to whoever it is. I don't want you working there anymore. I don't want you involved or caught up in anything that could put you in harm's way." He watched her eyes dart around the kitchen before her shoulders slumped and she sighed.

She looked slightly uneasy, but she could only guess that it was the news of her silent employer.

"I'm out of milk. I could go downstairs and get some," she frowned thoughtfully then.

Wesley fixed her with a weary look. "I'll go. You freshen up and just calm down. I love you Kristen. You can trust me too. I just want the truth. Do you love me enough to tell me that?"

No, she thought, even though she nodded slowly.

It wasn't that she didn't love Wesley with all of her being; it was losing him with the truth that cautioned her.

He walked over to her from around the kitchen counter and gave her a deep kiss. "Trust that," he said while taking her into a steely embrace. He let go of her quickly, remembering her bruises.

As if reading his mind, she cupped his face. "It doesn't hurt that much."

He walked over to the door then and fixed her with enquiring eyes. "Do you need anything beside milk?"

"No," she shook her head. "Just hurry back."

The reassurance in her voice made him relax even more. He smiled the littlest smile before closing the door behind him.

Outside the building, the morning had heated up somewhat. Wesley bought milk and the newspaper from a corner shop, and a bunch of yellow tulips from a young girl who was trying to sell them to motorists from the traffic island. Just for a moment the activity had distracted him from what had unfolded in Kristen's apartment a few minutes ago.

He was anxious to learn the connection between her and Vito Goliath, apart from the fact that they both spoke Italian fluently.

Wesley spied the mourners leaving the cathedral. He'd just have half hour at the most before he'd have to get back to the office.

The lift seemed to take forever. By the time he got to Kristen's apartment, he had already read half of the front-page article. It had faces of supposedly notorious gang bosses slapped all over the page. Someone was allegedly masterminding offing all the local drug lords. Quite rightfully, he thought.

He opened the door and stared at the empty spot on the floor where the maroon suitcases had been.

Before he even called or set out to find her, Wesley already knew in his gut that Kristen had lied to him.

She was gone.

# CHAPTER SEVEN

*Cape Town Central SAPS, Caledon Street, Cape Town*
*Wednesday, 26 March 2008*
*17:30pm*

Kieran hated the intensity of Police Commissioner Captain Zeldré Miller's round face. The strict uniform she was dressed in accentuated her lean, muscular body. An official officer's hat hid the short greying crew cut that emphasised the no nonsense attitude the woman was so famous for. Huge hazel eyes bore into every pair of eyes when she spoke and when she didn't. Zeldré's full mouth was a permanent stern line. She was a perfect poker-faced cop whose colleagues called her the *Intimidator*. Her expressionless face gave nothing away. She threw the Cloete file onto the table in a manner that was perfected over years of practice. The contents of the file were evenly fanned out on the table in front of the group of top cops from across the province. "Something is missing from this file, gentleman. This is not the complete file I've had delivered to this precinct."

"My men are working on finding the culprit, Ma'am." Kieran offered. "We believe that whoever took the info from the file is either working for Van Sitter or is being forced to do it by another drug lord."

It wasn't a good enough answer for her. "Have you been locked out of your own head, Clarke?"

There was a whisper between the men that came to an instant halt when Zeldré scanned them in a heartbeat. "Seven merchants have been killed off in the Mitchell's Plain area since February," she didn't have to consult the report and crime scene photographs in her hands. She knew them by heart. "Four in Elsies River. Five in Bishop Lavis. Three in Kensington. Four in Lavender Hill. Four in Eerste River. The list goes on and on and on.

"I want to know who is giving the order. I want to know who else is on that hit list. I saw a front-page article with that bastard Van Sitter being shot in the arm. I want to know which hospital he was at. I want to know which SAPS branch took his statement. Nothing has been sent to my in-tray and it's been three days since that article was on the front page. Today's leading story makes me wonder whether this city's police are competent at all."

Kieran ran a hand through his hair. His neon blue eyes were dull and bloodshot. Decent sleep would have fixed that, but the constant stand-by and stakeouts were starting to take its toll on his body.

"The latest update from the coastal towns, are that most of the criminal activity that has suddenly flared seems to be drug related," Zeldré paced slowly. "It appears that the bulk of indecent assault, pick-pocketing, theft, smash and grabs, stabbings by scissors… screwdrivers… bottle necks – and, my new personal favourite – nail files are all the work of youths under the influence of illegal substances."

"We've sent a team out there. No one in town knows anything about any merchants who have come on the scene. There is nothing new – at least no one is talking about it," Kieran Clarke flexed his shoulder muscles. "Surely a team can be put together by the *Criminal Juvenile Investigations*. They're the only hope we have to get into school benches. School starts coming Monday. That gives CJI enough time to plot."

Zeldré nodded thoughtfully. "I've already spoken to Detectives James Allen and Maxine Timm. A team has already been doing some groundwork, so rest assured, we'll have something by the start of the new school term."

Zeldré Miller and Senior Superintendent Fred Lloyd headed the Criminal Juvenile Investigations, or CJI for short. The section was started as a pilot project by the National Department of Defence two years ago. Its mission had been to uproot crime and criminal activities in and around schools countrywide. This undercover operation and secret unit functioned from a safe location that no one, except members of the elite squad themselves knew.

The team of internationally trained intelligence experts was a success purely because the field workers could all pass for teenagers.

Kieran knew only two of the team members who worked on CJI, simply because Detectives, Lee-Ann Barry and Alexandra Hugo used to be his best crime fighting duo before they were snatched by Zeldré.

"So far, all they've come up with, Captain Clarke," Zeldré fixed her cold hazel eyes on Kieran. "Is that the few smugglers in these towns are only a drop-off point. As it turns out, the head of two of the totalling five establishments has lost their bosses in the latest killing spree among local kingpins. That means that all the leads they've gotten has led them nowhere. And, as you suggested, a team will be taking up class space by the start of next week." Zeldré scanned the room one more time, making certain she met each and every pair of eyes that stared back at her with full attention. "I don't have to say that if this info leaks from this room every head will roll and you'll find yourself in a nice confined prison cell with all the criminals you've arrested over the past ten years. Do I make myself clear?"

"Yes ma'am!" it was a simple unison of voices that made even Kieran's spine stiffen.

Zeldré paid them no attention as she gathered her belongings, and left the room without a sincere gesture.

When he was alone in his office, Kieran pulled the outdated newspaper closer to him. He studied the profile pictures of the deceased drug lords and made a swift discovery. The photographs in the paper looked familiar because it was pick-up pictures from his SAPS files. He checked the by-line of the article and fumed. *Crime Reporter*, it said. No other name. There was only one person who could have gotten hold of his documents.

He slid his mobile out of his breast pocket and dialed Helgar Swain.

## *Krimson Kimono, Greenpoint, Cape Town*
## *Wednesday, 26 March 2008*
## *18:00pm*

Helgar sat staring at Wesley after she'd hung off with Kieran.

At that exact moment, Natasha had placed a large plate of hot curly fries between them and brought Wesley a second beer and a fresh martini for her. She gave Wesley a questioning look before leaving the table.

Surely she didn't think that he was cheating on Kristen with a journalist, did she? Wesley had called Natasha when he'd first discovered that Kristen was missing. She had sounded just as shocked as he.

There was nothing he wanted to keep secret from Natasha since he had picked up that she was very close to Kristen. She had, after all, been the reason why he and Kristen had ended up in his car the night at the Stuffed Pineapple.

"That was Kieran," Helgar raised the glass to her lips and slurped deeply. "He warned me that if I interfere one more time with any of his investigations by going through his documents, he would arrest me."

The look on her face told Wesley that Helgar was convinced that her boyfriend wasn't kidding this time around. "Did you? Go through his documents?"

She stared at him over the brim of her glass. "I'm a journalist. I tell things the way they are. It's my job to be the watchdog for society." She shrugged and leaned a little closer to him while she popped two fries into her mouth. Wesley had told her about Kristen's sudden disappearance that had her suspicious.

"I've been in here late yesterday afternoon," she said in a lowered voice that only he could hear. "It turns out that one of the waitresses had given some posh doctor Kristen's student number. I called the campus and apparently my contact at the university noticed that her e-file was opened some time last week, right after the waitress claims to have given the student number."

"Why a student number?"

"That was the only information this place has of Kristen Katts. I tried talking to the manager, but she insisted that she didn't remember anything about that day until – guess what?"

"Tell me," Wesley took a slug of his beer.

"The Premier had been in here with a *weirdo* and a *polished* middle aged woman with an English accent." Helgar rolled her eyes. "That was a direct quote, so by the way."

Wesley's mind raced. "The Premier? Wasn't her daughter on the list that you said was found on Jacques?"

Helgar's smile was sly and sheer pride, "Exactly. What I'm waiting for right now is confirmation from the City of Cape Town to tell me who has ownership of this place," she tapped a finger on the shiny table as she spoke. "Whoever the owner is, or the rental contract belongs to must have something to do with the Italian Mafia. I tell you, Wesley. Whoever is responsible for those Montello bullet shells in your apartment and at your parental house, owns this place."

Wesley sighed. "I've asked her… I've begged Kristen to stay away from here."

Helgar nodded thoughtfully. "What did she say to you before she left?"

"Just that I had to trust her. And, that I had to stay away from Vito Goliath, who happens to be my boss."

"He is the one she argued with?"

"In fluent *freaking* Italian!"

Something stirred in Helgar's eyes.

Wesley hadn't mentioned to her before that Kristen had been arguing with his boss in fluent Italian. Could it be a coincidence?

"Look," she said trying to sound neutral. "I'm being sent to Hawston for a few days to check out a location that one of my contacts had tipped me off on. Say as little about this to Kieran should he approach you. Wesley please… Kieran cannot know what you've learnt from me, and especially, what I've learned from you."

## Hout Street, CBD, Cape Town
## 21 April, 2008
## 12:40pm

The weeks had dragged by slowly.

Kristen had disappeared without a trace. The Baxter had no record of her having loaned any props. She had not made contact with any of her friends or with Natasha.

Every call he had received from a number he didn't recognised or a hidden identity had set his heart racing and had his stomach in knots.

But, none of the calls were from Kristen.

The news about circumstances surrounding Jacques Cloete's death had slowly died down. Lately, it got a mention in one or two drug-related articles, only stating that police were investigating and now and then someone had been taken in for questioning.

He'd been expecting Helgar back today. Wesley was certain that she'd been productive in Hawston, as news articles by *Crime Correspondent, Hawston,* graced the news pages of the daily English newspapers.

He turned his attention back to his work.

At first Wesley thought he must have been squinting. He checked the screen against the printout in his hand, and then checked the screen again, "Oh sweet lord!" Wesley gasped in terror.

He'd thought that he'd made a mistake earlier on when he'd come across a similar glitch, but his instinct was telling him that no glitch in the system could transfer 10% of seven figure amounts of money into a separate account.

There was something odd about the transfers. There was no indication of dates of time that the transfers had taken place. Wesley went down the entire list for a second time.

It seemed that somehow someone was transferring money from these new Swedish bank business accounts. The only explanation was that the account the money was being transferred into, must have been on the system as well.

The inconsistencies had never stood out before, but then again, maybe it was because he'd only really started paying attention when his computer codes were returned and changed a week ago. He'd been using Daniel Marcus's codes. The analysis of the system had kept him busy for more than a month, and finally, he'd had a break.

Whoever the culprit, was becoming impatient and greedy. Wesley had the feeling that if he just kept searching his computer, he'd find a lead. This guy was bound to slip up somewhere, he thought.

Wesley placed a call to Daniel Marcus's cellular phone. He told the older man of his discovery.

"Let's keep it between us for now, son." Daniel rambled off on the other end. Wesley could hear the hum of the traffic. "I'm just rushing to Westlake. There is a problem at the American Embassy."

"Okay, sir. Should I let Mr Goliath know?" He couldn't even say the surname without wincing.

"Not at this time. I will talk to you in a bit." Daniel Marcus hung up, leaving Wesley even more suspicious.

The ringing of his desk telephone made him jerk. He looked up at his screen and recognised the number.

"Dad," he smiled to himself. "I've just been about to call. How are you?" They were doing well. It was almost time for him to get his medication from the day hospital. He wanted to know whether Wesley could take him the following Tuesday. There was also some turpentine needed for a can of paint intended for the kitchen and the bathroom.

After his dad had hung up, Wesley stretched and yawned. He started on his admin for the helpdesk calls he'd received that morning. Just as he noticed his colleagues tidying up their desks for their lunchtime break, the phone rang again. And, again it was his dad. Only this time, he was being invited to supper. His mother was making his favourite roast. There were things that needed to be told to him. It would mean a lot to his mother if Wesley made an effort. They loved him, and he should have a good day.

By the time Wesley was done talking to his dad, the office had cleared out. He didn't really have anything to do in his lunch hour now that his girlfriend had disappeared from the face of the earth. He worried about her day and night. No one seemed to know where she was. Even Kieran had told him that she was not "missing" because she'd made arrangements to have her plants watered. There was however, something off about the way Kieran had suddenly become nonchalant about the case. He remembered Helgar telling him that he'd been a suspect. If he were a suspect, shouldn't he be questioned? Unless of course, he was being spied on or the police had already been on to the real murderer.

A telephone rang in the distance. Reluctantly, Wesley got to his feet and shuffled over to Daniel Marcus's office. Many calls filtered through to Daniel's office when his PA was out to lunch. And, thank heavens for lunchtimes because Mrs. Leary was a 60-year old Caucasian woman who lived for the day when the telecommunications giant delivered the telephone records for the month. Daniel had always kicked up a racket behind the drywalls of his tiny office when a call had either been missed or dropped. That usually happened on the 5$^{th}$ ring. Just as he reached the door, he heard the shuffle of papers before Vito's voice boomed from inside the office as he answered.

Wesley's eyes scanned Mrs. Leary's desk where each employee's name was colour coded in bold highlighted strokes. Each telephone call exceeding R2.75 was highlighted. The green highlighted telephone number caught his eye. He lifted the pile of papers to see who'd made the call totaling a hefty R83.70.

Vito Goliath.

The call was made to a telephone number starting with +27 28. A Hawston area code.

A strange coldness settled over him. Wesley checked further down the list. There were more calls made to the same number. There were also calls made to a guesthouse in Durbanville, which were highlighted too. He caught the name on the printout.

*Caribbean Blue.*

Cold shivers made his skin crawl. He could still hear Vito on the telephone behind the thin wall. He was once again speaking in fluent Italian. This time his sentences were curt, and not as heated as it was when he'd spoken to Kristen.

Kristen.

Wesley's heart gave a painful squeeze. If anything had happened to her... He couldn't even finish his own thought. The only thing that had stopped Wesley from confronting Vito and his link to Kristen was the look of outright fear Wesley had remembered in her eyes when she'd asked him to stay away from Vito.

*He can never know that you and I are together.* The sound of her strained voice echoed in his head.

Wesley took a deep breath.

He searched the contents of Mrs. Leary's desk for a pen and scribbled the telephone numbers on a pink post-it.

He heard Vito saying his good-byes, and quickly escaped into the foyer where he flew down the fire escape stairs two at a time.

Once he was outside the building, he loafed outside the building until he saw Vito pulling on a golf jacket and slipping into his nippy little Audi.

It didn't take Wesley very long to regain his cool. He went back up the stairs. There were fifteen minutes left of the lunch hour that he knew he could put to good use. If Vito Goliath was making calls from the office, he sure as hell was keeping notes and other correspondence around. Wesley had a hunch, and he knew it would some how lead him to Kristen.

It was now or never.

Wesley let himself into the office Daniel Marcus shared with Vito – when Vito had been at the office. He spun around on his heel before he noticed a brown leather briefcase stashed under a chair beside the steel filing cabinet.

Hurriedly, he fell to his knees and ran his fingers through the compartments. The inscription on the back flap told him the expensive sleek bag belonged to *M, VG*.

"Mr V.G," Wesley mused. Then he held his breath as he pulled a brown A4 envelope from a middle compartment.

He flipped the paper flap open and carefully pulled out the contents. It appeared to be correspondence from some or other pharmaceutical laboratory. He took a closer look. There was no email address on the bottom, but there was a fax number at the top that he'd missed with the first glance.

"Oh my God… What kind of business do you have going in Hawston, Mr Goliath?" Wesley stashed the documents back into the envelope and rolled it up to be easily slid into the sleeve of his shirt.

He checked the time; he had a few seconds to leave Daniel's office before the team rushed back into the office to continue the business day.

The day seemed to drag on slowly.

Wesley fought the urge to grab the envelope from where he'd slipped it into his own briefcase when Daniel walked into the office.

Daniel Marcus was a burly 42-year old divorcee with no children, and an ex-wife half his age. His dark eyes were deeply set in his round face and almost dwarfed by thick sooty brows. His Indian heritage from his mother's side stood out boldly in his make up.

He cast a look upon Wesley that meant only one thing.

"Uh-oh!" Wesley nodded as though reading Marcus's mind, "Trouble." He rose from his behind his desk and followed the boss into his office.

Marcus was seated behind his neatly organised desk when Wesley reached and closed the door behind him.

"We have a massive problem, Mr Johnson."

"I'm all ears, sir." Wesley handed the printouts of the problems he'd picked up earlier to the overweight man on the opposite side of the desk. When Daniel made no attempt to take the documents from him, he simply set them down in a neat pile beside the folded hands of the boss.

"It seems as though someone has been using your passwords and codes to transfers hefty obscene amounts of cash into an offshore account, Mr Johnson. Would you care to explain that to me?"

The door opened and closed behind him. Kieran Clarke and two uniformed officers he'd never seen before stood on either side of the door. Wesley shot a questioning look at his boss, "Sir? Surely you don't think that I could have -"

"Used your codes to transfer information to an account that checks out to your name?" Clarke interrupted.

"I have only one bank account. And it happens to be a local account." He pulled a notepad from his pocket and handed it to Clarke. "These are the times the transfers in question were made. I have an alibi for all of them. Besides, the last time I used my own codes was the day I got bashed over the head with an elephant's ass."

"Don't get clever with me, Mr Johnson," Daniel groaned. "It will be a shame to lose you as an employee, and by God, I admit that you are my finest employee. But, this —" he handed a printout to Wesley with all of Wesley's personal information and a life policy as collateral on the electronic contract. "Do you mind explaining to me how you managed to get into the building to make all of these transfers to your Swedish account?"

Wesley took a few deep breaths. Anger would make him ramble and say stupid things. Instead he reached for control and spoke calmly. "I don't have an off-shore account," Wesley began. "Did anyone bother to check the date the account was opened? Did anyone bother to verify with the bank in question whether they have telephonic recordings of this supposed account? We are the helpdesk. If any calls were made and deleted from this system, the call should still be on the Swedish records. That is the way the system was designed. In the data of the call, you would be able to determine the satellite location of the call." Wesley pulled out a chair for himself and sat down, his confidence taking over and clearing his mind of everything, except lateral reasoning. "Once that is confirmed, you are free to check it against my alibis for those specific times."

Clarke turned to one of the officers. "Hlubikazi," he extended a hand. "The file?"

Wesley and Daniel watched as Clarke paged to the beginning of the file. "Mr Johnson. You said in your statement that you needed a request for a new set of passwords on the day you were mugged here in the office. Why would you need new passwords if you use the same passwords everyday?"

Daniel cleared his throat, thoughtful brows drawn together. "He'd just received his passwords for the month. We'd just had a routine scan of the system to check for viruses and any spyware."

"I see," Clarke turned questioning eyes to Daniel. "So, who else had access to Mr Johnson's password?"

"No one," Daniel said. "The system automatically selects a password and sends it to our cellular phones. We received it just before lunch on that day. I remember that because," Daniel's voice caught in his throat. "I was at the Family Court with my wife. Ex... ex-wife."

A guarded look settled over Clarke's features. He turned his attention back to Wesley, who had started to look really bored, but as neat as a pin. "You reported your cellphone stolen. Did you have any time to write down the codes somewhere?"

"No. No one touches my cellphone. When the system is down, I use it as a modem."

"That's true," Daniel said looking at Clarke with accusing eyes. "That was the whole purpose why Mr Johnson and I are the only two in the building with a password."

"If Mr Johnson was attacked in the office and nothing was reported missing but a cellular phone, couldn't it be that the culprit's intention was the passwords on the cellphone?"

"That's true," Daniel angled his head apologetically at Wesley. "Can you think of anyone who –"

Clarke shut the file with a loud clap. "Jacque Cloete."

Daniel and Wesley turned to the police Capitan with twin dumbfounded expressions.

"It says here in Cloete's statement that he offered to help you with some or other problem on the PC?"

"Yeah... It wasn't the first time he offered. But that still doesn't explain the transfers from the past two weeks," Wesley rubbed his chin thoughtfully. "Unless-"

Clarke shook his head in realisation. "He was working for someone else. A spy or a drug lord maybe," Kieran Clarke was a man whose mind ran out ahead of him. "Do you have an alibi for your whereabouts when the last miniscule transfer was made Thursday after Easter?"

"Yes," Wesley nodded. "I was with –" Helgar Swain. Darn it! He couldn't do that to either Helgar or Kieran Clarke, even though he was the one drilling him at that instant. "I was with the afternoon crowd at a sports pub in Greenpoint called the Krimson Kimono."

"Can anyone vouch for your presence?" Clarke prompted.

"Yes. The manageress, Natasha. And, I used my credit card to pay the bill," Wesley spoke without hesitation. It was amazing how he could recall every day after Kristen had left. His days and nights were so empty that the entire day kept playing over and over in his mind. He heard Clarke speak with accusation lying just beneath the surface.

"What were you doing at the Krimson Kimono, Mr Johnson?"

Thanks to Helgar, Wesley knew that the place was under surveillance for weeks. "I was hanging out. My friends and I have been going there since it opened five months ago. You can go there alone as a young man, Captain, and meet up with new people all the time."

Clarke nodded thoughtfully. He turned to the uniformed officer beside Hlubikazi. "Simms. You can put that notebook away now. I think that's all. Unless," he motioned to Daniel and Wesley, "you have anything you'd like to add?"

Wesley sat at his desk a half hour later watching the closed door to Daniel's office. The police officers were still in there with the boss man even after he was permitted to leave. He burned to peep into the box he'd found behind some other boxes under the desk that once belonged to Jacques. He'd snatched it while Mrs. Leary wasn't at her desk. The box was labeled *Jacques Cloete Desk* in a thick black marker.

By the time everybody was packing up at home time, the door had not yet opened at the other end of the office. Wesley threw his blazer over the brown box and hurled it under one arm, reaching for his satchel with the other.

Mrs. Leary's head was still down when he left the office. A pile of telephone statements lay sorted and highlighted with the next day's date placed below each worker's name. He almost laughed once he entered his apartment a few minutes later. His colleagues sure had a lot of budgeting to do to repay or explain their telephone accounts.

A quick shower and a healthy balanced meal were rewarded with a beer when he eventually settled himself in the middle of his bed in a navy blue dressing gown. He pulled the box closer to him and was almost too afraid of what he might find. But, after almost an hour of nothing but telephone messages and emails and black and white printed photographs, Wesley relaxed slightly. In his attempt to get the circulation going in his sleeping foot, he accidentally kicked the box over. Its remaining contents spilled over his lap.

A black pocket-sized notebook stood out between the white and yellow pages. He opened the book with care as though the contents in it might be strewn with an invisible toxic substance.

"This could be it," he said out loud, though the only other sound apart from the loud rock music from the apartment next door was a dripping tap in the kitchen. He paged through the book, not knowing what he was looking for in particular. Jacques's untidy scribble was near illegible until he froze at a splash of red ink. Below it was a number he recognised as an international mobile number. The name below it was one that sounded vividly familiar.

Anne Thomas.

*Tango-Hippo-Orange-Mango-Apple-Strawberry.     First    name: Apple-Nectarine-Nectarine-Elephant.*

Reality hit him like a ton of bricks. His memory was suddenly as clear as day. Whatever made Kristen disappear was linked to Anne Thomas. He remembered instantly the night they met at the revue bar that she had mentioned her Italian heritage. Wesley ran a hand over his face. But what did Kristen have to do with Vito Goliath? And what did Vito Goliath have to do with Jacques Cloete's murder and disappearance? And, most importantly, "Who the hell owns the Krimson Kimono?"

There were two people who could possibly know. Wesley neatly placed everything back into the box, stashed it into a cupboard and threw on a pair of jeans and a polo shirt.

One thing was certain, and that was that Anne Thomas was an employee of Lutzio Montello.

He slid into a windbreaker, already dialing Dianna. By the time she'd agreed to meet him and hung up, he dialed Helgar.

He heard the exasperation on the other end. "Read the paper tomorrow. It's a feel-good story, but read between the lines," Helgar whispered into the phone. I have the feeling that the particular laboratory mentioned in tomorrow's paper has a lot more going on than the Premier is letting on."

"Turns out that your boyfriend no longer thinks I'm a suspect."

"How so?"

Wesley gave her a run down of the day's events that led him to that very moment.

"It could be something, but then again, it could be nothing. I haven't heard anything from my contact at the registrar's office. That'll be the first thing I do when I get back. We'll nail the asshole who owns that swanky little Krimson Kimono. I guarantee you that. Once that's out of the way, we'll find Kristen."

It wasn't good enough for Wesley, but he agreed and set off to Observatory to meet Dianna.

# CHAPTER EIGHT

*Rondebosch, Cape Town*
*21 April 2008*

It was a long day of auditions.

Dianna and Freda sat outside the theatre on a wooden bench with foam cups of coffee and muffins. Things had become extremely tense at varsity with Kristen gone.

The two girls were worried bout Kristen after they had no luck finding her or hearing from her.

"It's so bizarre!" Freda stared out in front of her. "She got someone to *water* her plants?"

"The only plants Kris has are cactuses," Dianna sighed heavily. "I just hope that wherever she is, she's safe."

"Yeah," Freda nodded. "I hope so too."

The shadow that suddenly fell over them caused both girls to squint.

"I thought I'd find you here," Wesley's voice sounded. "I think I know what might have happened to Kristen."

Freda raised a brow as she perked up. "Well?"

"I had a call from a journalist by the name of Helgar Swain a few weeks ago. She is a crime reporter –"

"Yeah, yeah, yeah! Get to the point!" Freda snapped.

"There is an Italian national called Montello who is some A-list drug lord, working with a local guy. Last month, I had a call for bookings on a flight for two from New York to South Africa. One ticket was for someone named Lutzio Montello. The other was for Anne Thomas."

"Anne Thomas?" Dianna and Freda turned to each other in horror. "Do you remember that British woman who came by the auditions and asked Siraaj some in and out about Kris?" Dianna's shrieked in panic.

Wesley's heart slammed furiously in his chest. "What did he say?"

"Just that she lived in the CBD. The woman had a British accent, so we all supposed that she was a relative of Kristen's," Freda picked at her muffin.

Reality blew like the wind. Wesley's gut knotted. "When was that?"

Dianna tilted her head to allow for stray curls to fall out of her face. "That could have been around Easter time. In fact, it was the day that Dylan introduced us in the club."

"Are you sure?" Wesley asked. "That was the Thursday before Easter."

"Maundy Thursday," Freda said.

That was also the day he witnessed Jacques being murdered. And it seemed clear. "Vito Goliath must have ties to Lutzio Montello and Ann Thomas. If that is true and Anne was looking for Kristen, all she had to do was give her name and cellphone number to Vito. He could have traced Kristen like a deer with his knowledge of computers," Wesley's head pounded. He thought back to the Good Friday morning when she'd told him that she'd slipped in the bathroom. "Oh Lord!"

"What is it?" Freda jumped up from the bench.

"I think Kristen was kidnapped by Vito Goliath," he said.

A voice behind him made them all jump. "That can't be," Helgar said as joined them hastily. "She handed Wesley a notebook. Vito Goliath is running checks to find Ms Katts also. Let's hope we find her first." She turned her attention to Wesley. "You need to find someone who has access to the registrar's office. If we can find the owner of the Krimson Kimono, we may be able to find Kristen. She must still be in the country."

"How do you know that?" Wesley asked.

"No one by the name of Kristen Katts has left the country in the past few months," Helgar said. "I've checked with the airlines and Customs."

Dianna cleared her throat. "Does Dylan not work with permits for establishments like the Krimson Kimono?"

Wesley wagged an enthusiastic finger at her. "That's right! I'll call him."

"He will be right here in a few minutes to pick us up," she said.

Freda turned to Dianna. "I'll go grab our bags inside."

Wesley watched as Freda sprinted towards the building. "Helgar, I think someone may have surveillance set up around places and people Kristen knew."

"No. The police would have known that," Helgar sighed.

Just then, Wesley's cellphone rang. "Johnson."

Helgar and Dianna watched the colour drain from his. The two women froze.

Wesley hung up.

"I have to go," he said.

"Where to?"

"Strandfontein. My parents may be in danger."

Helgar raised a crooked eyebrow. "Why?"

"Someone just told me that I made a big mistake telling the police about the irregular transfers on a client's account."

"Work related? Was it Vito?" Helgar asked.

"No. It was a local accent."

"Male or female?"

"Male. He said he needed my word that I'd leave my codes in a white sealed A4 envelope in my parents' mailbox, or there would hell to pay."

"Hell to pay?" Dianna frowned. "Why at your parents' house?"

Helgar grabbed hold of Wesley's shoulders. "Get over there right now and get your parents out."

Dianna flung herself at Wesley, holding him in a fierce hug before allowing him to back away.

When he drove off, Dianna turned to Helgar.

"You know more about this than you're letting on, don't you. This is about Kristen, right?"

"Yes," Helgar said in a no nonsense tone. "I just got back from Hawston. I don't know how much Wesley has told you, but I'm going to brief you."

Dianna nodded.

"I came across lab just outside the little coastal town. The laboratory belongs to a local drug merchant named Percival van Sitter."

Dianna nodded. "I've heard about him before."

"I've been tracking local paper reports and came across the name Dr Anne Thomas," Helgar continued. "Anne is a British national. It turns out that the good doctor has a working permit for Italy, Russia and the USA."

Dianna frowned thoughtfully. "How did you get to that information?"

"With the help of contacts at Home Affairs and Customs. I'm a journalist, Dianna. I have contacts everywhere," she winked. "Now listen closely. Wesley was right about the connection between Anne Thomas and Lutzio Montello. The old man has a son who my Italian embassy contact has informed me, is known as a heartless beast when it comes to assassinations for the Montello Empire. Our local police made the discovery that Montello has a daughter right under our noses. Apparently this woman owns the Krimson Kimono where your friend Kristen has been working."

Tears filled Dianna's eyes. "Do you think Wesley could be right? That Kris was kidnapped?"

Helgar shrugged. "I don't know. There are so many things that don't make sense. The puzzling thing is that Lutzio's son – and this I haven't told Wesley – is a partner in the firm that he works for. Vito Goliath is in actual fact Vito Montello, second name Goliath."

"But Kris is British."

Helgar raised a questioning brow. Her big green eyes seemed glassy in the rapidly fading sunlight. "How sure are you of that?"

"Pretty sure. She's got British academic credits."

"Has Wesley told you that he witnessed Kristen arguing in fluent Italian with Vito Goliath?" Helgar searched the younger woman's eyes.

Dianna shook her head. When she spoke her voice became very spirited. "What are you trying to say? That Kris has some kind of ties to the Italian mob? And just because I speak fluent French or Freda speaks fluent Russian, that she has ties to the Russian mafia?"

Helgar reached for a cigarette and a lighter in her bag. She made quick play to light it, took a long drag, exhaled. "It is confusing isn't it Dianna? Why would Vito Montello leave Kristen Katts alive after a heated argument with no visible witnesses?"

"I don't know! But Kristen is not a drug addict if that's what you're implying!"

"I'm not implying anything Dianna. I need to get to the bottom of this so that I can help Wesley to find her. It's just a matter of time before the police find out what I know. And trust me, if Kristen is hiding something, they will find out," Helgar said before she spun around and walked over to her car. "I have to go. I have a deadline. If you can think of anything that will help us find Kristen, please, call me. And, don't tell Wesley what I told you about Vito Goliath Montello."

Alan's car pulled up as Helgar drove off. Dylan got out the passenger side.

Dianna ran her fingers through her hair in frustration.

"Hey gorgeous!" his arms stole around her. "I missed you."

Dianna welcomed Dylan's kiss. "What took you so long?"

"The clutch cable snapped. Alan was kind enough to fetch me." He looked over her head to see Freda sprinting across the courtyard toward them before hearing her scream out in pain.

Dianna tore herself away from Dylan and ran over to Freda who had folded to the ground. "What happened?"

Freda rocked back and forth holding her ankle. "I think I may have sprained it."

Dylan was careful in picking her up and carrying her to the waiting car, with Dianna following with two sports bags.

The car was a mess, Freda noticed. It was in serious need of a vacuum even though it smelt of expensive masculine cologne.

"Alan, this is Dianna's friend Freda." Dylan turned to Freda, "Alan is a doctor. He'll take a look at that ankle when we get to my place, ok?"

Freda nodded. "Thank you."

Alan gave her a backward glance. "Sure. Nice meeting you."

Once they drove off, Dianna beside her in the back, Freda touched her ankle. "It hurts like a bitch..." she turned slightly to Dianna. "Hey, what's wrong? Why are you so quiet?"

Before Dianna could answer, Dylan's cellphone rang. He was talking in quick sentences of Afrikaans before turning his attention to Alan, who gave him a sidelong glance.

"Strandfontein. It was Wesley. The Johnson's house is on fire."

Dianna held her breath and reached for Freda's waiting hand. How did things turn out like this so suddenly?

### Strandfontein, Cape Town
### 21 April 2008
### 19:42PM

The house was already in flames when he arrived less than an hour ago. Thick stubborn smoke curled heavily in the darkened sky. Sirens and fire engines sounded around him, but Wesley could feel nothing. He was incapable of doing anything.

The only sound that played over and over in his head was his mother's agonising scream that seemed to pierce through the night as bystanders witnessed her flaming, blistering body pressed up against the burglar bars of the burning house. Her clothes had melted into her flesh like plastic. She'd reached out through the bars where the heat of the fire had caused the windows to splinter into the crowd with a forceful explosion. He had run toward the house, wrestling firefighters as he tried to get to his mother. Her skin had already turned to charcoal and the piercing scream had gotten softer.

Alan and Dylan were there suddenly; tackling him and dragging him back seconds before all three turned to the burning house to witness something that would haunt them forever. The trapped woman went completely silent. The next moment a loud crack followed a gruesome explosion of the human head that once belonged to the woman who had been a mother to all of them.

Dylan had dragged Wesley away to where he now sat staring at the house from the back seat of Alan's car. A paramedic had seen to the three young men.

Freda leaned her head against Wesley's back. The splint around her ankle had allowed the pain to settle somewhat. Dylan had been soothing a crying Dianna a few feet away from Wesley.

"Are you okay?" Alan's voice was shaky as he leaned into the car.

Freda nodded. "I'm okay. How is…?"

Alan followed the trail of her eyes to Wesley's back. "Not well at all. You want to come out here for a second?"

"Sure," Freda managed a small polite smile. She turned to Alan as he closed the door. "This has got to be so traumatising for him."

"For us all I'm afraid. Mrs. Johnson was like a mother to Dylan and me. Mr. Johnson was living proof that you could have the best fun with a limited cash flow."

Freda turned her attention to the black ruins of the Johnson's house. Medics were leaving the house with stretchers and body bags.

She shook her head. The overwhelming grief the suddenly gripped her had her sobbing uncontrollably. Before she realised it, Alan was holding her. Her arms moved in their own accord as they went around his neck.

Freda wasn't certain how long they'd stood there comforting each other, but a police officer was suddenly beside them. He stretched out a hand to Alan.

"Captain Clarke," Alan said as the two locked hands.

"I'll just get back in the car, if you don't mind." Freda excused herself and struggled into the back seat of the car. She could hear the muffled voices outside the car. Wesley was still sitting with his back to her.

Freda sighed. Her eyes scanned the car until she noticed a soiled envelope ear sticking out beneath her feet. She reached down and wrestled the manila envelope out from under the seat.

Staring at the Premier's address on the front, she pulled out one of the documents. Her eye fell on a name she'd been hearing a heck of a lot today. *Dr Anne Thomas.*

She carefully unzipped her bag and slid the envelope inside, without taking her eyes off Alan and the police captain. Freda watched closely as Kieran Clarke handed Alan a small dark box. "Make sure Wesley gets this. It was found close to his father's body," Freda heard him say to Alan.

### Cape Town Central Police Station, Caledon Street, Cape Town 30 April 2008

He knew Zeldré Miller's team had been on to something when he saw the thick police file under her arm. Her expressionless face told him that there was a heck of a lot going on.

Today she had insisted on meeting with him alone. "My kids on CJI compiled this interesting report," she pushed the file across the table to him. "The laboratory in Hawston has gotten the stamp of approval by Wilhelmina Langenhoven. From what Detective James Allen and his partner has gathered thus far, is that the lab not only houses young homeless youngsters, but the skill they are taught is all about turning cocaine into heroine."

"Heroine?" Kieran fell back in his chair. "Where is it coming from Zeldré?"

Zeldré Miller wiped a hand over her face. "Nigeria. There is a *rendezvous* point there. The coca is manufactured there once it arrives from Thailand. The plantation in Thailand belongs to the notorious Lutzio Montello."

"That doesn't explain what Montello is doing in Cape Town."

"Kieran… Why was Jacques Cloete murdered and where was the body found? We need to find the local merchant Montello is working with. Jacques Cloete was a supplier who wanted out. But his drug habit kept him tied to the mert responsible for his death. We find out whom he was working for. We find our local man. I have a team of experts working inside that lab as drug addicts. I want your men to withdraw."

Kieran was on his feet. Fire flashed from his blue eyes. "You can't be serious! This is my area!"

"No! This is my area! And that was not a request Captain Clarke! That was a direct order. Your girlfriend is quite a distraction isn't she? And, if my pictures end up in the paper one more time, I'm going after her. She is a danger to herself and to my staff. Helgar Swain is going to be the death of many members of the police unit."

"Leave her out of this," Kieran barked back.

"Withdraw your men."


## Cape Town International Airport, Cape Town
## 22 May 2008

It had come like light at the end of a tunnel when his mobile rang that morning. Home Affairs had called with news that there was movement on Kristina Katherine Montello. The daughter of the notorious Italian mobster had left the country on Thursday, 27 March. After eight weeks the airline company had called ahead to confirm their list of crew and passengers due to arrive late afternoon from a straight flight from Amsterdam. *Kristina K. Montello*, Italian National had her name printed right between a local sport personality, *Nadine S. Moller* and a senior South African National *Janice Y. Montgomery*.

Surveillance teams had been quickly setup at the airport, along with airport security and police personnel posing as porters and airline staff. An officer was placed in the airport's customs office that would evidently be one of the first people to spot the Mafia Princess.

It had taken longer to set up the operation than he had initially thought as the official end of the tourist season had finally arrived.

Kieran stared through the panoramic windows at the airport as the massive airplane landed and a mobile passage was attached to the door of the craft.

The earpiece crackled in his ear a few minutes later.

*"We have movement on the Trinket. Trinket is carrying a single red carry-all as hand luggage."* The voice over the earpiece crackled and then the connection faded.

It was easy to spot the red bag. The Mob sure made certain that their princesses were kitted in the latest fashion off the Milan catwalks. Dressed from head to toe in the hottest Italian brands was Miss Montello. The only reason they knew it was her was because their guy posing as a porter, had patted her on the arm and said, "Welcome back Ms Montello."

She wasn't as tall as he had thought she'd be. In fact, Kieran was disappointed that the woman was not as stick thin and tall as the Italian models he'd seen in his monthly GQ magazine. From her profile that wasn't hidden by a hat or by her flaming brown hair, he could tell that she wasn't as old as he'd initially thought. He consulted the copy of her passport they'd gotten from home affairs. He checked her date of birth and gaped. Kristina Montello was only twenty-three years old.

It happened all so quickly from that moment on. He raised his binoculars to his eyes. Although he knew that she couldn't see him, Kristina K. Montello looked right at him. The coincidence made his heart skip a beat. He recognised her instantly.

She was the student who Wesley Johnson had reported missing just over a month ago. Kristen Katts *was* Kristina Katherine Montello.

The question he asked himself now was whether he should keep that information to himself, or whether he should trust Zeldré Miller enough to use the Montello girl as bait to lure out the big fish.

The less people knew her true identity the better. Kieran was already convinced that Wesley had no idea who his girlfriend really was. However, with his knowledge of IT, it wouldn't surprise him if he were well on his way to making the discovery himself.

The police team moved like clockwork. Every woman and man in Kieran's employ carried out his and her part as smoothly as possible.

Kristen had been well aware that she'd been followed. She was an old dog to Interpol and elite crime fighting forces. Though, she had to hand it to the South African police. They had a good game of cat and mouse going. She'd known something was up when a random passport check was carried out. It was so obvious that the man and his supposed partner had waited for her to be at the mouth of the plane before he gave her a friendly slap on the arm and pronounced her name so legibly that even she herself had been tipped off as the crackle from a listening device had sounded in his partner's ear. There was an upside to her life, she supposed.

Going back to the CBD was a bad idea.

Whatever she was suspected of doing, she didn't want Wesley involved. It also occurred to her that her apartment might have been bugged, or worse: her father or brother had set up surveillance to monitor her every move. If that had been the case, Wesley was out of harms way since she'd left.

The porter who assisted her from the point where she collected her luggage was too stiff and professional to be a regular. The woman didn't even chew gum for crying out loud. Kristen almost laughed. She pulled out a crisp blue banknote and handed it to the girl. "Here you go," she smiled. I don't have smaller. Guess it's your lucky day." Kristen smiled her most sincere smile. She knew that a well-trained cop would take the money. She was already convinced that the woman was no porter. But the hesitant hands of the woman told Kristen that she was new at being a cop or it was her first undercover operation. "I don't have smaller than that," she repeated.

The woman touched a hand to her ear, and then nodded. She reached out a hand and took the crisp bill. "Thank you," she mumbled, pulling the luggage trolley along.

By the time Kristen had checked into a hotel near the airport, she was exhausted. She wondered why the police had been following her. The weighty scenarios she'd thought up were making her nervous. Whatever it was, police knew she was somehow tied to Lutzio Montello.

*Oh God, please... Wesley cannot find out this way.*

Kristen sighed. She'd rather have Wesley meet someone else than have him know her true identity.

Kristen was only too aware of what he'd thought of the crime underbelly that she'd been born into. The look of pure hatred that flashed over his face when he'd mentioned the owner of the Krimson Kimono was a mafia princess had haunted her for weeks.

*He can never find out.*

# CHAPTER NINE

*Canal Walk Mall, Milnerton, Cape Town*
*12 June 2008*

The brightly lit shopping mall was abuzz with parents stocking up for the June school holidays.

It was just a matter of time before she would run into Wesley. Avoiding him had been the worst part of her return. We would have learned by this time that she was back. She managed to survive the past few weeks without running into him, but the newspaper she was clutching in her hands had a huge advertisement on the back page with her and the rest of the *Soweto Day* cast. She hadn't been quite ready to face Dianna and Freda. The last fourteen days saw her running from the theatre at every chance she got. She'd avoided them like the plague. The only contact she'd had was Freda grasping her shoulders on stage and just before the director yelled for them to cut. She'd given Kristen a quick: "What the hell is going on? Where the freaking *hell* have you been. Why are you avoiding us?"

"I can't explain…" is all Kristen could get out before breaking out of Freda's grasp and fleeing the premises. There were worried glances passed between Kristen and her two best friends all of the time, until last night when Dianna had broken into tears.

She'd looked at Kristen with so much compassion, that Kristen could no longer shy away. It wasn't a complete fabrication of the truth, but she'd managed to make them promise not to let Wesley know that she was back.

She knew that Freda hadn't bought her story one bit. Neither did Dianna, but Dianna was too polite to question. Freda had simply rolled her eyes and said: "Horse shit!"

"Okay," Kristen had said. "It is not the whole truth. I was in Italy. I've also been in Pretoria."

"*Tswane*," Freda interrupted, folding her arms over her chest and raising a brow. "It's not *Pretoria* anymore, you know. The TV news is already calling it *Tswane* – not that government has officially paid the nineteen billion of the taxpayers' money to have it changed or anything."

Dianna had poked the dark-haired girl in the ribs, and tried desperately hard not to laugh.

"Okay," Freda rolled her eyes once more in jest. "Call it *maar tog* Pretoria."

If there was one person who could even make even the Queen's guards laugh at Buckingham Palace, it was Freda.

"What were you doing in Italy?" Dianna asked with a slight confused frown.

"I've applied for citizenship in your country," Kristen's gaze moved between the two of them.

"But you're British. Why would you want South African citizenship?" Freda asked, seriously this time.

Truth time, Kristen had thought. "I'm not British. I'm Italian. I've been schooled in Britain and lived there for a while." It wasn't as if she'd told them this bit about herself before. They'd assumed based on her polished accent that she was a born and bred English lady, and that was not her fault.

"Italian?" Freda had asked in sheer surprise. "Italian as in *Luigi pasta bon ici ma?*"

Kristen's eyes scanned the newspaper in her hand as she remembered the intense conversation she'd had with her two best friends.

She flipped it back to the front page, blindly scanning the picture of a blazing building.

The thought of Freda's face at the answer to the Italian question had Kristen shrugging presently in the paperback store.

She'd told them about the South African arts student she'd met on the Spanish Steps in Rome. It was amazing at the rate the walls around them had broken down and the bonds between the three of them had immediately become strengthened over coffee and cinnamon buns.

Then again, there was no place in the world that quite made cinnamon buns like the Silvaro Hotel in Rome. That's where she'd had coffee with Benedict Forlani. Benedict. The memories of the weeks in Italy made her smile. He was a postgraduate student inspired by water. His obsession with water features had taken him to Rome where he painted every fountain on his canvases that had many tourists offering him hefty amounts of money for his work, but he was saving his masterpieces for his debut art exhibition at the *Le Artist* restaurant, doubling as a gallery, in the mall.

The friendly Benedict had tried to engage her in a romantic relationship, but settled rather to be an ear and a shoulder to cry on when she'd needed it. Now that they were both back in South Africa, things would certainly be more bearable with just one person who accepted her the way she was - a black market good.

Wesley was almost certain that the woman at the paperback shop was Kristen. He'd heard from Dianna that she was back. From the lack of movement at her apartment, it was obvious that she was staying elsewhere. With the spare key still in his possession, nothing had been moved or taken from the apartment either. He'd called every hotel, guesthouse and lodge he could find on the web, but she wasn't listed as a guest at any of them. Every search he'd attempted to find her whereabouts had come up empty. Only names closest to hers had been kicked out. The search was becoming frustrating, even more so since he knew for certain that she was in Cape Town.

Since the company had landed a new contract with a car hiring service, *Ryder-Delle*, Wesley had taken the past three days to re-programme and get their system launched.

The particular job had brought him to the entrance where he'd seen a Kristen-look-alike glide out of an art shop. He followed her into an arts and craft store, ever observant of her moves. But, she had wide designer sunglasses on her nose, which made it pretty hard to identify her. He was certain that her voice would give her away, but it was as though she could read his thoughts, the only voice was that of the elderly cashier who rang up a few tubs of glitter.

He'd lost her then. She couldn't have gone far, but yet she was nowhere in sight. She had disappeared in the five seconds it had taken him to leave the shop.

After nearly half an hour of searching, he gave up and made his way back to Ryder-Delle.

His heart sank, his blood running cold in his veins.

The woman behind the desk was explaining to her that her international license had expired. "How you managed to use this drivers license to purchase a car before is already an offence, ma'am." The navy blue suit of the service consultant was striking against the young woman's soft features. Her dark blonde hair was tied back in a severe French braid, as she went on and spoke to the elegantly dressed woman across from her. The sleek black linen suit accentuated her curves as she adjusted the red scarf from her head to her shoulders.

In a slow, almost practiced movement, she turned and met his gaze from over the brim of her sunglasses. Every trace of colour washed out of her face, leaving her chalk-white. Her eyes were pools of bottomless green panic, as she stood there, motionless.

It seemed like more time had gone by than the solid minute it took before the service consultant cleared her throat. "I'm sorry, ma'am. We can't help you."

"That's alright," Kristen spoke in stifled whisper. She took back her license and threw it into her bag. Her heart raced as she forced herself to move to the door where Wesley stood, arms folded and watched her like a hawk.

"When were you going to tell me Kristen? I had to hear from small talk that you've been back nearly three weeks."

"Wesley... I... can't we –"

A baritone of a voice behind them made them turn in unison. "There she is!"

Wesley turned his attention from the formally dressed man to his runaway girlfriend. He fixed her with questioning eyes.

"Darling!" the tall, dark man reached for Kristen's shoulders, but backed off immediately when Wesley's arm snaked around her waist.

"You have about ten seconds to explain why in the hell you are calling my girlfriend 'darling'." Wesley gritted his teeth.

Kristen took a sharp intake of breath and moved between the two men. "Wesley. This is Benedict Forlani. He is an artist. He has his first exhibition right here at the mall. Benedict, this is Wesley Johnson. My boyfriend."

The alien tone of her voice when she said "boyfriend" caused his grip on her to tighten, making her flinch.

"How is it that you know Mr Forlani, *darling*?" Wesley mocked.

"We met it Rome," Benedict offered. He turned his striking hazel eyes from Wesley to Kristen, giving an impish little smile.

"Rome? What were you doing in Rome, Kristen?"

This was not the time to have this conversation. "Can we talk about this later?" Kristen shifted uneasily.

Wesley jerked his head in her direction. "The last time I agreed to leave a conversation for *later*, you disappeared. Now it turns out that you were in Italy for heaven's sake."

Benedict cleared his throat. "Trust issues are so last season, man. Now," he looked from Wesley to Kristen. "Would you please come along? I have an exhibition to set up."

Kristen gave Benedict a small smile. "I'll be right there."

"The hell you will!" Wesley peeled.

"Hey man," Benedict backed up. "You don't own her."

"And you do?" Wesley challenged the other man.

"It's her choice. Isn't it? I mean... if you love your girlfriend, surely you should trust her."

Wesley let her go abruptly. The movement was so quick it rendered her off balance for a brief second. She turned back to Wesley and spoke in a whisper so that only he could hear her. "Won't you come with me? I promise, I'll tell you everything after the exhibition."

"Kristen…"

"Please. I will tell you about Vito Goliath and why I had to go to Italy."

"What about why no one could find any trace of your existence after you disappeared?"

Kristen held her breath before exhaling in one leisurely rush of cool air. "Yes."

"Right now, I'm convinced that you are not Kristen Katts. So if you're not, who are you?"

She moistened her suddenly dry lips before looking him square in his guarded brown eyes. "I promise you, I will tell you." She didn't really have a choice. Two things were certain. One – Wesley did not know her true identity. Two – if she didn't come clean about it, he would find out soon enough. One call to the car rental agency could give him clarity on that. The risk she was taking had her stomach in knots once again.

The knowledge of her being a Mob princess would not be taken well by the one man who had shown her true happiness. Kristen knew deep down that the gnawing in her gut meant that telling Wesley the truth meant that things would only end badly, but she loved him and the only hope she had at that moment was the faith in the love he had had for her.

### Shortmarket Street, CBD, Cape Town
### 12 June 2008

The drive into the city was a tense, silent one. Kristen was aware of Wesley's sidelong glance every so often.

He knew she was awake even though her eyes remained closed behind her dark glasses. There were a million questions swimming around in his mind, but he instinctively held back the urge to ask them. He'd seen the tense look on her face when she told him at the art exhibition earlier that she needed to sleep. She made it clear that she would not be returning to her apartment and that she needed to check out of a guesthouse in Newlands.

Wesley had insisted that she stay with him. That was when he turned to her in the brightly lit gallery and noticed the fading bruise at the corner of her eye. There was more going than Kristen would allow him to know. He knew that now, cutting the engine in front of his apartment but leaving the wipers to swipe away the heavy rain that had battered the windscreen.

Neither made a move. Wesley gave a backward glance at her luggage. He was happy to see the maroon trunks had been exchanged for modern trolley cases in a brilliant shade of red.

She sighed. "I didn't say thank you."

"You can say thank you by telling me what you were doing in Italy. And, why you refused to see me. Does it have anything to do with that Benedict guy?"

Kristen didn't take her glasses from her face when she turned to him and spoke. "No. It had to do with me. I had some unfinished business."

"In Rome?"

"Yes. I've applied for citizenship in South Africa."

Wesley ran his fingers through his thick dark hair and let out a long breath. "I thought you were kidnapped. I thought something bad had happened to you."

Kristen's breath caught in her throat when she turned to find that his eyes had become over emotional. He was trying desperately to blink them away. "Wesley," she sighed, flinging the sunglasses from her face and onto the dashboard. "I didn't know how to talk to you after that last day in my apartment. I thought that I could just leave and never come back, but I'm so sick of running." The effort it took to say those words out loud brought stinging tears to her eyes. "I don't want to run anymore... but I do need time."

"Why?"

"You'll have to trust me, Wesley."

He shook his head. "Too many things have happened Kristen. I want answers. I deserve answers. I was a wreck after you left and then..." he still couldn't talk about his parents. He swiftly changed his line of thought. "And then you come back and tell me you want us to be apart? That is what you're saying isn't it?"

Kristen made a frustrated sound and flung her arms around him.

Several silent minutes went by before he gradually worked his arms around her. It was as though he was afraid that once he'd held her like he did in his dreams for so many weeks, that she'd disappear and he'd wake up in a cold sweat. The frustration, the anger and the hurt fused together until he could no longer stand it. He pulled her away from him so abruptly that she gasped in fright. Her chin was tilted inches above his mouth. "If you want to tell me something, tell me that you love me and you'll never leave again and I'll forgive you Kristen. I'll forgive you."

It sounded like a desperate plea instead of the request it was meant to be.

Kristen knew she could not let this go any further until she told him the truth, but she was powerless against the touch of his lips against the underside of her jaw. Her pulse raced and all rational thoughts had been smothered by the desperate, hungry kisses Wesley was sharing with her.

The effort her overexcited body took to make its way into Wesley's neat apartment felt as though she would burst from frustration. The door latched automatically once he'd pushed her back against it and started working her free from the black suit that held the heavy scent of her exotic perfume. The sleek black linen suit accentuated her curves as she adjusted the red scarf from her head to her shoulders.

Wesley crushed her against the door with his body. The fierce longing in his eyes as he raked her face sent her heart slamming in her chest.

# CHAPTER TEN

*Strandfontein, Cape Town*
*12 June 2008*

It was going to be a cold night.

The temperature had dropped from an afternoon 25 degree high to a 13-degree high overnight. The chill in breeze was a sure sign that winter had arrived in the Mother City.

Through the window of his luxurious Strandfontein home, Percival Van Sitter watched the thick band of clouds descending down heavily over Table Mountain.

His luck had taken a downward spiral lately.

The nosey journalist and the troublesome cop kept turning up like flies in his ointment.

Now that Vito Montello had found a suitable candidate to frame for Percival's business deals with the Montello Empire, it was smooth sailing all the way to the shores of San Jose. He always had dreams of retiring from the world of crime and starting up a beach bar like he had seen in the *bioscope* many years ago when he was still a boy with ambitions far from the career path he was racing down now.

He had admired Lutzio's son, who was his age and yet a hitman for his father's empire. Vito Montello was a bastard that spared no mercy for his victims. Percival had witnessed the satisfaction in the young Montello's eyes as he watched the long and painful suffering of the elderly couple in a house a few blocks away.

The hit was carefully planned. A series of small mini explosives were setup at strategic points of the house causing an electrical fire to blaze at all exit points of the single storey house. The fire had blazed through the house rapidly and caused instant destruction to everything in its path, and doubling in size every seven seconds.

The moment the heat had blasted glass splinters into the narrow Mitchell's Plain road, firefighters on the scene had no hope of saving the couple pressed against the burglar bars.

The smell of searing human flesh had stayed with him when he had joined the gathering crowd outside the burning house. Percival had not imagined that the *hit* the Montello's had planned would be as gruesome as what he witnessed that fateful night. He didn't have the stomach for it. He remembered the amused grin Vito had briefly snuck him when his stomach rolled and he spewed all over his new branded sneakers and the front of his jacket.

"Is something the matter Percy? No napkin?" Vito had mused.

"You are an animal," Percy said.

Vito had shaken his head. The flames from the fire up ahead had made his eyes glow. For a long moment, Percy thought he was staring into the eyes of the devil himself. "This is no way to off anyone, especially not an innocent couple."

Vito shrugged. "We want to frame their son. There should be no family ties when he is in jail. He should have no one waiting for him. Your men have kept a close eye on him, si?"

"Ja. No girlfriend, just a few regular friends."

"Well Percy," Vito slapped him steadily on the back after the local gang boss had another spew, this time hitting his baggy jeans. "I do hope that your men know what they are doing. You have a problem with the way I work? I hope you could teach me a thing or two about offing people."

Percival had been mocked. He wiped his mouth with a swipe of his arm. Just because you have to kill, doesn't mean your assignment has to suffer and be tortured.

Vito smacked his lips together and cooed in another gesture of mock. "Ahhh..." he tilted his head at his local counterpart. "You don't honestly care about these people do you?" Vito nudged him. "You sell them drugs to support their habits. You just take out those who don't support your business. Make an example of a few people. Who is going to remember their names in a few weeks? You remember Jacques What's-his-name? No? I didn't think so."

Percival grabbed his knees the third time his stomach rolled. He lifted his head and scanned the scene. At the front of the house two other men were holding by a young man back forcefully. "Is that who we are framing for the accounts and the stash?"

"Yes Percy. That there is Wesley Johnson."

Thinking back to that conversation had made Percival's stomach roll with nausea again. Vito Montello was not a man to challenge. It was only a matter of time before the police would close in on Wesley Johnson. By the cruel way Vito had murdered Wesley's family, Percival had masterminded a plan to save him from the hell that awaited him in prison.

By killing the young Johnson man, there would be limited evidence found in a police investigation that might prove the Johnson man had been framed. He would be doing Wesley a huge favour by bombing his car. It was fool proof.

This was South Africa for crying out loud.

All the justice system needed to save costs was to have someone to take the blame, limited evidence to stop the investigation and stamp it as a cold case. That's how he usually took care of a messy situation. The number of judges he had for clients was astonishing!

His thoughts were running away with him. He hardly heard the door open.

"Is it done?" Percival's voice echoed through his office.

The young man slouching in the door nodded. "*Ja baas*. The *manskappe* are still at that guy's *pozzie*."

"Did they wire the right car?"

"Yes Mr Van Sitter. The black *golfie* was in the parking bay. The men are watching the house."

Percival nodded thoughtfully, "Any word from the Montello's?"

The door flew open and revealed Vito Montello with three men following close behind him. "I'm right here Percy." He held up a high tech laptop computer before placing it on the massive oak desk. "I thought we could watch the fireworks in Shortmarket Street from here. You did say that you could teach me a thing or two. So let's hear your step by step guidance."

Vito was deliberately trying to provoke him. He knew that. Percival was also wise enough to know that starting a fight with Vito Montello at this sensitive stage of their deal would end in a bloodbath to his own disadvantage.

Instead, he forced himself to give a hearty chuckle. He turned to the young man who was now presses against the door, obviously intimidated by the three masculine men flanking Vito Montello in their matching leather gear and semi-automatic weapons.

"Donny! Organise Mr Montello a *dop*!"

Without hesitation, the young man stumbled out of Percival's office.

### Shortmarket Street, CBD, Cape Town
### 12 June 2008

The aftermath of their lovemaking always felt like the most sacred part of being with Kristen. Wesley marveled at the way her limp body melted into his. Her hair, damp and curling, covered his arm that supported her against his length was pure satin.

The subconscious way she nestled her cheek against his naked chest made his blood soar despite the physical impossibility of making love to her so soon again.

Her sleep induced voice crackled, bringing him to full attention. "What are you thinking?"

Wesley chuckled lazily, stirring. "I'm just mesmirised by the woman who has turned my life upside down." Wesley felt the sudden tension that made Kristen's body rigid for a few seconds before she relaxed again.

He eased her away from him gently and flipped onto his side, facing her.

"You scared me when you disappeared. I thought you'd been kidnapped, Kitty."

Her lashes swept up as she stared into his dark eyes. "What made you think I'd been kidnapped?"

Wesley sighed. "So much has happened since you've left. Dangerous and complicated things happened that still doesn't really make sense. There are British doctors roaming around and," his voice trailed off by the alarm that flashed in her green eyes.

"British doctors?"

"Yes. It's a woman. She's been asking about you, Kitty."

When she rolled onto her back, and sighed deeply, Wesley propped up on one arm. "I won't let anything happen to you Kristen. There is just one thing I need to ask of you."

She opened her eyes and stared at his now serious face, free of humour. "You cannot go back to the Krimson Kimono."

"Why not?" She frowned. Irritation edged her usual sensual tone.

"It turns out that the pub is owned by an Italian mob princess."

Kristen's sudden bleak face made Wesley uneasy.

"Kristen," he pleaded as she rolled out of bed. "This is serious."

"You know Wesley, maybe you are just reading too much into rumours. She reached for his shirt and pulled it over her lush naked body. "Where do you come on this nonsense?"

"It's not nonsense," he followed her into the bathroom where she was already stepping into the half-filled tub, scrubbing away at her body almost immediately. "The police are all over Greenpoint. They know who she is."

"Why are you telling me this?" Kristen grabbed a towel, wrapped it around her and stepped out of the bath.

"Because I don't want you caught up in any of this."

Too late, Kristen thought.

"I just want you to be safe."

Kristen spun around and looked Wesley square in the eyes. "I can take care of myself Wesley Johnson. I don't need a male nanny!"

Where was this sudden attitude coming from? "Kristen, I'm not saying that you cannot look after yourself."

"Then what are you trying to say?" Her spirited voice caught Wesley off guard. His own voice had taken on a harsh undertone. "I'm trying to tell you that I care about your safety. You are not just some girl, Kristen! You are the one woman that I want to spend the rest of my life with!"

Now, fully dressed, she grabbed her bag from a chair in the tiny living room. "You have a goddamn funny way of showing it!"

"Where is all of this coming from?"

Kristen ignored him as she yanked her snazzy mobile phone from her bag. "Dianna? I'm at Wesley's. Is there any way that you can be here in time? This rain is killing me."

Wesley listened to the cold tone that made her voice almost unrecognisable. A moment later, she shoved the gadget back into her bag.

"The rain caused some flooding. Dianna can't be here in time even if she takes a detour. I'll call a cab."

Wesley pulled on his jeans and a T-shirt. "I will drive you."

"You will do no such thing! I don't want to be around you right now."

"What has gotten into you Kristen? It's not as if you own the Krimson darn Kimono!" He looked at her thoughtfully. "Unless you do know something that I don't?" He said. "Then again I would have known."

Her head snapped up. "And how would you know that? Did you go through my apartment looking for clues?"

"As a matter of fact, Miss Katts, I did. Yes, I went thought your things to try and find you!"

Kristen froze in horror. "You went through my personal things?"

Wesley's eyes softened. "I was trying to find you Kristen. Why does it matter to you? Do we have trust issues? I thought we had no secrets."

"I have to go. It's opening night. Will you let me borrow your car?"

Wesley shook his head in disbelief. "Are you avoiding the topic?"

"No. We'll have to pick it up later."

"Why don't I believe that later won't ever come?"

Kristen sighed, grabbed the car keys from the coffee table where he had tossed it earlier that afternoon.

Reflexively, he countered her, snatching the bunch from her. "I'll drive you."

"No!" she wrestled with him, on the verge of tears. "I don't want you with me!"

"I'll drive you!" he was almost desperate to calm her down.

Get your hands off me!" she pushed at his chest. The effort won her a stumble from him. That tiny moment of weakness from Wesley won her the opportunity to grab the keys. Before he completely recovered, Kristen made for the door and stumbled out into the late afternoon storm.

Wesley took after her. They were both instantly drenched by the pounding rain. Despite his anger, he felt his gut knot and his heart squeeze when her eyes locked with his in an apologetic gesture before she got into the car and slammed the door.

"Kristen!" He advanced to the car, his bare feet icy from the beating rain.

Then, as she twisted the key, the engine started up with a roar. The next moment an earth shattering explosion slammed him to the ground in a pool of water. A second explosion lifted his flaming car from the street, setting off car alarms all around.

The impact of his fall had impaired his ration. And then, it had hit him.

Kristen.

Kristen was in the car that had exploded into flames.


## Strandfontein, Cape Town
## 12 June 2008

Percival stared at the two men who stood in front of his desk. Vito stood with his back to them where he gazed out the window. The expression on his face was unreadable.

The plan had not gone accordingly. The two young men, dressed in twin black suits were visibly shaken.

"How sure are you of the identity of the woman?" Percival asked, his eyes rolling wildly between the two men.

"There was nothing we could do boss man," the slighter of the two handed over a badly burnt passport. "By the time we got the warning from Mr Montello, the girl had already gotten into the car," his nervous eyes roamed over the rigid man whose stance at the window oozed volumes of danger and irritation. Clenched fists dangled by his sides.

Percival folded his hands over his forehead in defeat. "I told you to make certain Johnson was alone. No love interest."

"There were none sir, not until today," the man didn't take his eyes off the dark Italian at the window, still silent and rigid.

"What do we do now sir?" the young man stammered.

The figure at the window turned on the two men in answer. "Now gentlemen," he spoke in a slow, Italian drawl. "You pay for the death of my sister. You die."

Percival felt the sweat run down his face in sheer terror. He was painfully aware that none of his men could save him if Vito murdered him in cold blood. There would be bloodshed in his house tonight. He shifted nervously in his chair as Vito moved slowly toward the two men standing in front of his desk. In one swift move, the Italian squeezed the trigger of the gun that seemed to come from nowhere. Percival watched in horror as both his men dropped to the ground. He raised his gaze slowly to meet Vito's shadowed one. He closed his eyes, knowing his fate was in the hands of the man who towered over his desk.

### *Rondebosch, Cape Town*
### *12 June 2008*

The theatre was already filling up.

Freda watched Dianna pace, dialing phone number after phone number. "Why isn't anyone answering their phones?"

"You don't honestly think that Wesley and Kristen are somewhere having coffee do you, Annie?"

Dianna rolled her eyes at Freda who was busy unzipping her bag. "I'm worried, Freda. The weather is really bad. I told you that Kris sounded really upset when I'd spoken to her earlier."

Freda turned her attention to her bag. She stared at the manila envelope in the bag for a few puzzled seconds before remembering the document she'd found in Alan's car.

"Oh sweet lord!"

Dianna turned to stare at Freda in surprise. "What is it?"

Both girls turned to the sudden crashing open of the dressing room's door. Helgar Swain stood gazing blindly at them. Her eyes were bloodshot. "There has been an incident. I think Kristen is in trouble."

Freda handed the stocky journalist the envelope. "That is an understatement Miss Swain. I think you need to give this to your boyfriend right away."

Dianna's mobile rang in her hand. She answered the incoming call from the Krimson Kimono, her eyes growing wider by the second.

"Bad news?" Helgar asked after Dianna had hung up.

"It's Kristen. There was an explosion," she managed to say before the room begun to spin and she passed out cold.

# CHAPTER ELEVEN

## Shortmarket Street, Cape Town, 16 June 2008

Lutzio Montello's hostile eyes focused on the zombie-like man who sat dressed in expensive clothes clutching a familiar looking gun in one hand and a bottle of fine scotch in the other.

His daughter had died because of this piece of human scum. How had his baby girl become involved with Wesley Johnson? How could his son not have picked up on their love affair?

Sorrow had Lutzio Montello crippled for three days. But, the world had to be prepared for his revenge. First on the list were Percival van Sitter's illiterate boys. They've planted a goddamn bomb in a man's car that was dating his daughter. What were the chances that his Kristen would be around the computer nerd?

A bullet through the brain would have been simple enough, Lutzio thought. Then again, if they hadn't even done their homework surrounding Wesley Johnson, as professional assassins would have done – study the subject – what were the chances that they wouldn't have tortured and raped his daughter before killing her as well?

That seemed to be the way things were done in this God forsaken country. Where did you ever hear that religion had no place in the school's curriculum? No wonder teens and youths were stuffing money into his local counterparts' pockets – and himself for that matter.

Right there and then, Lutzio decided the best justice on the man who had given his car keys to his Princess would be to be killed by his own conscience.

By the state of the apartment, it was clear that the young man was distraught by the death of his Kristina. And, quite right that he should be.

Lutzio knew the numbing heartache. He recognised it.

The poor bastard would pay for his share in Kristina's death in the worst possible way. Instead of killing him, Lutzio would drive him to the point where he'd put the trigger against his own head. He'd heard how Wesley didn't believe that Kristen was the daughter of a mafia boss. He'd told police that he didn't believe it. Lutzio had been on the crime scene when they'd questioned Johnson.

The body hadn't been pulled from the flaming wreckage at the time. He'd only just been informed that the body had been recovered and needed to be identified. The cops were closing in on Lutzio fast. Every airport and every harbour saw a pack of police. They were combing the streets of Cape Town in search of him. Vito had sent a distress message via a pusher to the guesthouse in Durbanville to warn him of his arrest. He'd been nabbed at the Hout Street office.

Lutzio waited until the young man's eyes focused on him. The burly Italian lifted his hat in a mock salute to the broken down man slumped in a couch. "The name is Montello. Lutzio Montello." He watched in satisfaction as the name registered in the other man's brain. "We haven't met, son. I'm Kristina Montello's papa." Lutzio gave a curt humorless chuckle. "Or... as you've come to know my multi-talented daughter, Kristen Katts."

Lutzio paced slowly when he spoke again. "I'm going to leave you with a little parting gift. Maybe you will join your parents and my daughter soon," Lutzio put a shiny .22 caliber in Wesley's right hand with a mock sympathy squeeze. He lit a long fragrant cigar before placing it in a makeshift ashtray from an abalone shell. It seemed to be a popular thing in this strange city, Lutzio noted. He gave Wesley Johnson one last look and with a quick line of Italian, he left the flat.

The last three days were a blur Helgar reflected as brought her nifty little white sports car to a screeching halt. It seemed that the news they were bringing Wesley may have finally been the silver lining they were all hoping it would be. The doors of her car flew open in unison as the three girls ran into Wesley's ground floor apartment. The door was unlocked. "Wesley!" Helgar burst through the small passage; kicking doors open as she went along calling out his name.

"He is not here," Alan said as he and Dylan came into view in the doorway. "We checked at Kristen's place and all the other places he could have gone. We didn't check the hospital since you all were there," Dylan sighed.

Dianna gasped in horror when she took the filth that was so unlike the man who had owned the apartment, "Something is wrong."

Freda peeked at her from over the kitchen counter. She held four empty bottles of scotch in each hand, raising it for Dianna to see. "You're telling me. Has he been on a whiskey diet?" she scanned the sink and the dustbin. "There must be over ten empty bottles here."

Helgar appeared in the lounge with Dianna, tapping her foot and taking in a deep breath of air. "He can't have gone too far. The place smells of fresh cigar smoke."

Freda joined them, lifting a makeshift ashtray from an abalone shell. "Looks like he didn't care much for smoking it."

"Wesley doesn't smoke cigars," Dylan sunk to his knees and studied the contents on the coffee table. "It gives him a headache." He noticed a tiny silver object lay beside a cup of stale coffee. He took it between his thumb and index finger, rising to his feet.

"What's that?" Helgar started forward to him. The journalist took the object and turned the little cylinder over in her palm. "It's a bullet shell. The marking on it is the emblem of an Italian mob family. Montello."

Freda's voice sounded close and made them both jump. She held a flat cartridge in her hand. "I'm no detective, but this sure looks like snazzy bullets to me."

"Montello?" Dianna asked. She turned to Freda in surprise, "Oh holy hell! We've it all wrong!"

Helgar's worst fear was confirmed. "The owner of the Krimson Kimono is the daughter of Lutzio Montello."

"What was the name on the lease?" Freda placed the cartridge down carefully.

Helgar sucked in a quick breath. "Kristina Katherine Montello." She looked from shocked girl to panicked girl. "Aka: Kristen Katts."

Freda shook her head in complete disbelief. "So if Montello was arrested, who was here with Wesley? And where is he now?"

"It wasn't Lutzio Montello who was arrested. It was his son, Vito Montello," Helgar reached for the vibrating cellular phone in her pocket. "Excuse me, I have to answer this, it could be a lead."

Freda and Dianna paced the small apartment in an excruciating silence, before Dianna froze.

"Annie?" Freda was on her guard. She followed Dianna's path of focus. An orange flashing light on the telephone handset indicated the receipt of a voice message. She walked over and hit the button. A rapid tone sounded before a familiar recorded voice rang out clearly.

"Wesley, this is Natasha again. I'm on my way to the hospital in Greenpoint. It's Kristen. She is alive. I couldn't get around to calling you sooner. She is critical and in intensive care. Call me when you get this message."

At that exact moment when Natasha's recorded message gave the hospital's details, Helgar burst through the door, heaving. "It's Wesley," she looked at the foursome who held identical horrified expressions.

"He called? Is he at the hospital?" Dianna clasped her hands over her eyes.

Freda's arms flew around Dianna's shoulders.

"There is trouble in Long Street. We have to move now!" With that, Helgar backed out of the apartment. "Let's go!"

The road was clear most of the way.

"What's that sound? Is that sirens I hear?" Dianna asked from the back seat where she sat squashed between Freda and Dylan. Seconds later blue and red lights flashed up ahead, washing fear into the occupants of the car speeding toward the news breaking scene up ahead.

# CHAPTER TWELVE

*Long Street, CBD, Cape Town,*
*16 June 2008, Youth Day*

"Wesley!" Freda watched in horror as Wesley sat on his knees in the rain. The drains in Long Street had always clogged up so quickly once the rain carried the debris onto the concrete drain covers. It had made a puddle around him. She was pushing her way through the crowd. Fighting off a fireman as a police office shouted some warning at her. She had to get to him. She could see the grayish blue colour of his face. He was as good as dead. She heard an ambulance near by, but she knew no miracle could save him. With a frantic scream, she broke free and ran toward him. Water splashed and swished around her ankles, as she got closer to him. "Wesley!" she dropped to her knees. "Oh my God! Someone, help!" She sandwiched his face in her hands. "Wesley please… you have to hold on," Freda was shrieking as she searched his empty eyes. "Wesley! It's Kristen!" She saw something stir in his eyes. He was looking into her eyes as the gun dropped beside him. Blood was still pouring from his mouth. He reached for her hand with his.

Freda cried out louder in frustration and helplessness. She watched him mime "Kristen" as a question.

Freda nodded frantically. "Kristen is alive. She is recovering from her burns Wesley. She made it. Natasha tried to call you. You didn't answer –" She was being pulled away from him. She was being tossed aside. "No!" She screamed as she tried to get up. But exhaustion had got to her. She lay there in the rain with her face almost drowned in water from the road. She watched as Wesley was loaded onto a stretcher and hastily rushed into the ambulance. A flash of colour caught her attention. It was Dianna. She was running across the road to her with an officer in tow. Freda recognised him as Captain Kieran Clarke of the Cape Town Central Police Service. He shook his head in disbelief. "I'm sorry. I was so busy trying to hunt down Van Sitter that I completely forgot about the file."

"You forgot?" Freda rose in one smooth motion. "You FORGOT!" She was toe to toe with the Captain. Pushing and nudging him as she said, "That man was an innocent man!" she pointed in the direction the ambulance had sped away. "He had a breakdown because the South African Police Service is a joke! You had all of this information and you didn't check it out." She was clutching at his shirt as though she could tear it to shreds. "This would not have happened if you just listened." Freda let him go as she fell into Dianna's arms.

Dianna's tearstained face was seamed with exhaustion. She looked up to find Helgar Swain crossing the street toward them. Helgar's eyes were bloodshot, and her hair a red frizzy cloud. She shook her hair in irrevocable shock. Her gaze moved from Dianna's, to Freda, to the captain where it settled. He mouthed her a drawled out 'I am so sorry' before one of his constables appeared at his side and his attention had moved back to the job.

# CHAPTER THIRTEEN

## Plattekloof, Cape Town
## 17 February 2009

The rehabilitation clinic in Plattekloof offered the most exquisite views of Table Mountain and aerial views of the greater part of Cape Town. Kristen learned that she'd been at the two-story establishment the last eight months. Six of those months saw her in an induced coma. She was recovering from a series of surgeries to eliminate the scars the explosion had left her. She had suffered severe tissue damage and first degree burns that took months of treatment to reverse. When she had come out of her coma three weeks after the explosion, she'd thought that she had been badly deformed. The pain was too much and it was decided that keeping her in a medical coma might have been the only way to reduce the pain.

She remembered everything before the accident.

The last memory she had of that horrific night was her smelling the singeing of her own flesh and her scourged hair. It was the ruthless raw pain of the rapidly forming blisters, together with the maddening zinging in her ears that caused her to blackout, but not before by some miracle she'd flung herself from the blazing car. She still heard the sound of the sizzling puddle that had put out the furious tongues of fire that had nearly killed her.

Kristen shut her eyes tightly as she remembered the guttural roar that filled the night. He hadn't seen her fall out of the car. She had seen him from beneath the car; the second had seemed to go on forever. He was sitting on his knees huddled in a ball of sorrow.

He howled her name over and over again.

Seeing him down on the ground forced her to fight. She willed herself to survive. The second explosion hadn't allowed her any sympathy when it flung her whole world into darkness. But now, as she watched the sun set bathing the mountain with orange and crimson reflections, she touched a hand to her bandaged face.

Another week would determine whether she'd need more surgery.

She'd learned that her hair had been shaven off completely when paramedics found her. It was the storm that had saved her when she had gotten soaked outside Wesley's apartment. The drenched clothes that he begged her to swop with dry ones before she was supposed to head out to the theatre. Freda hadn't called. Dianna was too far away to make it to Wesley's in time. And then, Wesley had insisted he'd take her with his car. Wesley. The memory of him brought stinging tears to her eyes. She blinked hard when a rap at the door made her sit up rigid. It was the first time since being at the clinic that she was allowed a visitor.

In her peripheral vision a familiar shape came into view. The smell of summer filled the room. She watched as Natasha seated herself carefully in a wingback chair. She was wearing faded blue jeans and a black T-shirt. Her hair was pulled back from her face with an elastic band. "The nurse says the last of the grommets were removed yesterday. I bet hearing isn't as painful anymore."

Kristen watched as Natasha's hopeful eyes raked over her. She had forgotten the sound of her own voice. Disappointment had replaced so many of her emotions. Wesley hadn't come to look for her. His name was never mentioned by any of the people who frequented her room.

Kristen managed a nod in Natasha's direction.

"That's good," she gave a small smile. "The doctor says you'll need some more skin grafts on some visible places, but that the chance the laser treatment will restore the pigment damage on your face is high. Another week and you might have one more session."

Kristen remembered the doctor had told her himself that the skin graft might leave rough or dark patches but with regular treatment it would go away. She nodded again. There was more news in Natasha's eyes that caused Kristen to be on high alert. "Don't lie to me anymore Nat. Just tell me where he is. Where is Wesley?"

Natasha's gaze dropped to her knotted hands in her lap before she looked up into Kristen's questioning eyes. "Kristen..." her voice was broke under the strained remorse. "Wesley was shot."

Kristen felt ice creeping into her veins. The whole room seemed to be spinning out of control. Nausea strangled. All the furniture had turned into blurry dark shapes that knocked the breath out of her. She heard a ruthless roar escape her own throat. The ripping force of it made her sensitive throat feel raw and bruised. "*NO!!*" She heard it again. "*NO! No! No!*"

A sharp sting in her shoulder caused heat to surge through her body. The injection was calming her down almost instantly. The shallow breaths that puffed out of her eased some of the wild images that raced through her mind. Beside her were two nurses and Natasha was sitting beside her on the opposite side of the bed; holding her to her chest. She was cooing her. "It's okay. He *didn't* die. He is alive."

"I...w-want t-to see h-him," Kristen stuttered as she forced the words out breathlessly. She could feel Natasha nod before her voice sounded close to Kristen's ear, "Of course, Kitty. But you have to get well first. You need to get healthy again. You don't want him to see you like this."

Kristen managed to take a few deep breaths before plucking up the courage to ask. "Does he know I'm here?"

"No," there was no hesitation in Natasha's response. "He does know that you survived the explosion though."

Kristen's gut twisted in pain that made her cry out. She felt Natasha's arms tighten around her.

As if sensing the silent questions, Natasha said, "He hasn't come for you because he is unable to."

Kristen eased herself out of Natasha's embrace and lowered herself onto the twin bed. "I...don't u-understand."

"Kristen... that bomb wasn't meant for you. It was meant for Wesley. The guy behind it all was taken into custody and is serving a life sentence. The other men," she hesitated and her voice trailed off.

Kristen shook her head. "Tell me, Natasha. Please… I have to know who the other men were."

"It was Lutzio Montello and his son."

Kristen's eyes darkened. She felt as though her heart had been ripped out of her body. "My father?" she said in disbelief. "My father tried to kill me?"

"He tried to kill Wesley."

"What happened to *h im*? My father and my brother I mean?"

Natasha met Kristen's eyes. "They were extradited back to Italy. They were charged and are held in a in Rome until their trial has run its course. Apparently they were wanted in the States as well."

"The United States?"

"Your father and brother were notorious drug kingpins with empires right across the world. New York was where they used close to twenty tons of cocaine over two years to produce heroin. Your father had a coca plantation on one of the Indonesian Islands off the Timor Sea. Your father owned the island, apparently.

"They were doing business with a local drug merchant, Percival Van Sitter. They dragged Wesley into their criminal activities by framing him for all their monetary transfers.

"The company Wesley worked for was partly owned and financed by your brother. He used a different name, of course. It seems that one of Wesley's colleagues got hold of his cellphone and his diary the day he was mugged."

"That was the day I took him to the hospital," The memory was as fresh in her cloudy head as though it had happened yesterday. "I remember the surf rider with the blonde hair on the phone. He was weird. They found his body right after the Easter weekend."

Natasha nodded. "It's all linked. Wesley was framed for all of it. Your friends Freda and Dianna helped a journalist get to the bottom of it. They had given the information to the investigating officer, but he thought it was all taboo – obviously."

Kristen held her throbbing head. "He didn't use the information?"

Natasha shook her head. "No, Kitty. By then it was already too late. Wesley was already beyond any saving."

She was almost too afraid to ask. "What do you mean?"

Natasha smiled at her sympathetically. "I will tell you," she looked over at the two nurses who were rolling in a trolley with a healthy spread of food, "but you have to eat first."

Kristen nodded automatically and tucked into the small portions of the mini feast.

## Wale Street, CBD, Cape Town
## 04 March 2009

It took a week longer than the doctor had initially anticipated, but Kristen was ready to go home. Now that she was a multi-billionaire, it didn't seem right to keep money that had caused so many families heartache.

She dropped her carryall on the floor of her apartment before closing the door. The curtains on the opposite side of the room were slightly parted as she had left it. Everything else was in tiptop shape just as Wesley had left it the last time they'd been here together on the sofa. White sheets where now covering every last scrap of furniture throughout the apartment.

The South African flags waved proudly in the wind across the road of the Western Cape Provincial Parliament, a sight she associated with freedom when she first arrived in the Mother City. Now it was a reminder of the damage the vicious cycle a legacy of crime could do.

Kristen collapsed against the door, overcome with agonizing sadness, and howled. Would she ever heal on the inside like she was healing on the outside? She tried to get Natasha to help her see Wesley, but the response from the prison was always the same. Wesley had exceeded his visiting hours for the month.

Kristen forced herself to get up from the floor. She took the first wobbly step toward the first white linen sheet. She pulled it off the sofa with such force that it left her choking in a cloud of dust. The rush of emotions that flooded her was so severe; it almost knocked her to the ground. She braced herself against the backrest of the soft seat before pulling the next sheet off, then the next until all the sheets were strew across the floor of her luxury apartment.

Before long the apartment was as it was before and Kristen was refreshed. She traded her blue sweats for a jumper and a pair of jeans. Just as she was about to close the cupboard, she spied a black masculine suit jacket at the footboard of the cupboard. Before she could chicken out, she reached for it and figured that it had more than likely slid off the hanger. The overwhelming fragrance of Wesley's cologne reached her. It was feint, but lingered on the collar as she buried her face it and hugged it tightly to her.

An object in one of the pockets dug into her chest. She quickly pulled the garment away from her and patted it down. She sunk onto the floor as she wrestled with the button on the pocket. Her heart raced and her fingers trembled so much she could barely bring herself to stick her hand into the pocket. When she did, she found two things. One was a little note. She unfolded the A5 Irish margin sheet and read it out loud.

"*Son, we are truly blessed to have you. I'm just sorry that we didn't have the chance to say goodbye before we leave. Your mother and I are proud of you. It's time that we pass certain documents and heirlooms down to you, so use your key and take the parcel that's bound at the bottom of my sock drawer. We love you boy and we hope that you put that stone to good use. Your Dad'.*"

She let out a breath and stuck her hand in for a second time. It was a small box that felt strangely shaped. She pulled it out slowly and placed it in her hand before opening her eyes.

Horror flooded her. She studied the partially melted blue plastic box. A million explanations to its deformed state produced wickedly horrid images in her mind. She closed her eyes against the possibilities. A fresh wave of tears seeped through her eyes and fell onto her open palm that held the tiny box. She began opening it but it wouldn't budge. Kristen channeled all of her energy into one for pull. With a brittle but loud crack a three-tier ring set fell into her lap.

The yellow gold of the thin bands were gray from the fire damage. One of the three bands was a turn of the 20th century design. It was the most beautiful ring she'd ever seen. The diamond was flat and encased in a puckered claw that resembled a rose in full bloom. A knock at the door made her jump to her feet in fright. She ran over to her dressing table and took the contents of the jacket and carefully placed it in the drawer before taking a quick assessing look at herself. Yes, of course she looked like she's had a hell of a few months. Hell was putting it gently – not to mention the past two weeks. The sound came again and she managed to open the door with the door securely chained.

The familiar face of Captain Kieran Clarke held a solemn smile. "Miss Katts," he nodded. "I heard you've been released from the clinic. I just stopped by to see how you were doing."

Kristen stared at him in silence. She didn't move an inch. Captain Kieran Clarke was the reason Wesley was sitting in a jail cell somewhere, "How would you be doing if the roles were reversed officer?"

Kieran grimaced. "Not as well as you are." He searched her face, but it remained hard and stone cold. "May I come in? There are things I need to explain." After no response, he cleared his throat. When he spoke again, his voice was low and strained. "It's about Wesley Johnson, ma'am."

Kristen unchained the door and motioned for the handsome police Captain to make himself comfortable, as she followed suit.

"Miss Katts…"

"It's Kristen. Please."

Kieran nodded. "Very well. Kristen. Wesley is serving time for murder."

Kristen had already braced herself for hearing the story again. She nodded.

"He was cleared of all the other charges as the evidence showed that he was innocent.

"Mr Johnson did however shoot five innocent people; three of which were fatal. We didn't have a choice but to take him down. He was a danger to himself and to hundreds of innocent people.

"He was shot five times. They fought to keep him alive because of the bullet he suffered to the chest." Kieran shook his head. He buried his face in his hands as he exhaled heavily. He looked up again to meet her unfaltering gaze. "The bullet crushed his collarbone and did some damage to a cardio valve. The medical staff managed to restore it though. His collarbone healed nicely.

"He was unable to plead in the case, but a psychologist diagnosed him with reactive depression. And, therefore, he is to carry out four months of his eighteen-month sentence in Polsmoor. The other fourteen months has been suspended for five years. He also has one-hundred-and-forty-eight hours' community service from his release that has to be fulfilled within the first year." Kieran's solemn smile was back. "He ran into trouble with his cellmates, but we managed to move him into a single cell."

"What kind of trouble?" Kristen's voice sounded calm and steady – just the opposite of what she was feeling. It didn't just surprise her; Kieran gaped at her in shock.

He cleared his throat. "It was gang related. They assumed he was a member of the notorious 28's gang." He hesitated, "Things got rough. Wesley got hurt pretty bad. Nobody sent word to us from the prison. By the time I'd gone to pay him a weekly visit, I'd seen his injuries and gave the immediate transfer." Kieran gave a mock laugh that broke into a cry. "They now believe he is a police informant. The moment he is released, we're setting up a new identity for him."

All she heard was selective phrases. *Wesley got hurt pretty bad.* What that entailed, she was too afraid to ask. She lived in Cape Town long enough to know about the injustices that went on in state prisons. *Police informant. New identity.* Where did that leave her?

"When is he being released?" she fought herself to remain in control.

"Next week."

She shook her head in confusion. "I don't understand the timeline."

"He spent months in hospital recovering before the trial. So for the last four months he was in jail."

"I want to see him."

Kieran shifted uneasily. "That's kind of the reason I'm here. I have to ask you not to."

Kristen's head snapped up. Rage made her head reel.

"I told Mr Johnson that you made a successful recovery. I asked if he wanted me to bring you to him and he said –" he turned his eyes away from her abruptly. A muscle in his jaw flexed. His face was strained. "He said he didn't want to see you."

Kristen jumped up. "He did not!" she cried out. "He would never!"

Kieran was beside her. "I'm sorry."

"No!" she pushed at him. "This is all *your* fault and I don't care what *he* says! I WANT TO SEE HIM!"

Kieran nodded. "I'm sure I can arrange something."

Kristen swiped her tearing eyes with the back of her trembling hand. "Before he is released. I want to see him right now." She sniffed.

"That's impossible. But I can arrange for you to see him tomorrow."

Kristen sat back down and nodded fiercely. "Yes. That would be fine."

Kieran hesitated before talking, "There is just one more thing."

"What's that?"

"Lutzio Montello," Kieran watched her closely. Not a flicker of emotion showed on her face.

"What about him?"

"Is he your father?"

Kristen nodded.

Kieran unzipped his flak jacket slightly and took out a white overstuffed A4 envelope and handed it to her. He also gave her a small brass key. "It came for you from a woman named Anne Thomas. She was the one who took care of your father's clothing stores and fresh produce outlets in Italy and Spain."

"I know Anne."

"She paid your bills while you were in hospital. You do know, of course that all your father's narcotics establishments and its merchandise has been retained by the FBI and other international specialist units. Once the trial ends the bonds for the various premises will be turned over to you should the court rule otherwise. The island in Indonesia – that plantation has been destroyed. You are the owner of all his lands and legit businesses."

"What is so legit about anything my father owns, Captain Clarke? People have died. Families have been destroyed. Bloodlines have been tainted. Do you think I'm interested in any of it?"

Kieran shrugged. "What are you going to do with it?"

"I don't know," Kristen sniffed again.

"He wanted you to have it because of the accident. That bomb wasn't meant for you. And, he knows that he will be sentenced to death."

"No, it wasn't meant for me, but it would have killed me anyway."

He knew exactly what she meant. If Wesley had been killed in that explosion and she survived, the biggest part of her would have gone up in flames along with *him*: her heart and her reason for living.

# CHAPTER FOURTEEN

*05 March 2009*
*Polsmoor Prison, Tokai, Cape Town*

A prison warden dressed in khaki and green uniform escorted her down a long passage with a series of locked heavy barred doors. The smell of filth and pungent bodily odours made her stomach roll.

On either side of the passages, cage-like cells were jam-packed with criminals. The sound of her clicking heels and expensive feminine perfume had men rattling the bars of their cells. Cat whistles and offensive passes and comments sounded behind them as they made their way to the next locked gate. The burly black warden shrugged apologetically. "I'm sorry ma'am."

Kristen felt like a kitten in a dog pound. She must have looked it too since the warden had given her hand a reassuring squeeze. "They won't harm you. They can't."

Somehow she managed to swallow. And smile. "Thank you."

"This way," he said as he steered her through more aggressive and inappropriate passes at her. Just when she thought she would ask the warden to take her back, they got to the end of the passage. He led her down a tiny flight of stairs where the air was not as foul as before. He unlocked a solid door that led to a small lobby.

"He is already in there. I will be on this side of the glass," he pointed a window-like break in the wall. The room looked like a control room with a soundboard and microphones, cameras, computers and other little devices. "Clarke will be here in a minute or so."

Kristen nodded. She walked over to the window and looked through it with overwhelming sadness. The figure in the chair was sitting with his back to the glass. His shoulders were slumped forward in the bright orange prison gear. The round black prison identification stamps were closely printed on the thick cotton prison wear. Thick unkept black hair curled wildly over his collar. Kristen saw a thick matted beard before his profile was turned away from the glass again. She watched his shoulders square for just a few seconds before it slumped again.

The warden's voice startled her, "He can't hear you. He can't see you from here either. You have to go into that room."

Kristen froze. She'd come all this way and what she saw suddenly gutted her.

"I will be right her ma'am. If there is a problem, I will see and hear everything."

It was harder than she'd imagined. She took a step toward the metal door that led into the small room where Wesley was sitting and waiting. She pushed the door and waited – heart pounding – as the door closed behind her.

The room was even smaller than it looked through the window. The walls were a morbid gray. The threadbare carpet smelled of mould and dust. Two small mismatched padded chairs, of which Wesley occupied one, were placed across from each other on either side of a small wooden table. Her eyes dropped to the ground. She saw the chains around his ankles and the worn soiled Velcro-tie sneakers. She wasn't sure if it was white or gray.

He didn't move an inch.

Kristen started forward slowly.

His head was bowed down far enough for his chin to reach his chest. Thick hair framed his face. The man seated opposite her was a stranger.

Her aching heart pumped excruciating pain through her veins. She glanced over the bent head to where the window was supposed to be. Instead, she found herself staring into a mirror.

Her gaze raked over the swarthy man. His thick lashes swept his cheeks. Kristen shifted uncomfortably. She had laid awake all night trying to figure out what to say to him. By this time he would have heard the truth about her identity. A million lines swam around in her head – one's that seemed perfect last night. Now, however, with reality staring her in the face, they all seemed inappropriate. She burned to reach out and touch his arm, but she instinctively clutched her hands in her lap. And, then, like a thundercloud, she burst out, "What have I done?" It was a rhetorical question that was aimed at herself. She hadn't taken her eyes off him. He remained seemingly unaffected by her outburst. Kristen rested her elbows on the table and her hands sandwiched over her nose and mouth. She fought for control of her emotions, before she returned her hands to her lap. "I don't know what to say to you. I've dreamed of this moment for so long, but it just isn't the way I thought it would be," she stifled a cry. "Wesley…" Through the blur of her tears, she saw his eyelids wrinkle as he pressed them shut before they relaxed again. "Wesley?" her voice came out more desperate. "Please… Please look at me." There was no reaction from him. "Wesley, I have a lot to tell you and, a lot to explain about my family. About me…" Kristen's heart was breaking painfully slow. "I know you must h-hate me," She could hardly say the word. "But I want you to know that I'll always be in love with you. Even if you can't stand to look at me," her voice broke then.

Talking was going to be impossible, she knew, but she had to make him look at her. She needed to know that his eyes were not as empty as the ghost of the man he used to be, sitting opposite her. "I was angry with you," she started again. "When I learned that I was in the hospital. I was so angry because you weren't there with me. Not after I saw how devastated you were when the car exploded." Kristen didn't know what was more frustrating: talking about that fateful night or the lack of a response or reaction. "I fell out of the car, Wesley. I saw you. You were so near to me, but you were so far away at the same time.

"When I woke up in the hospital, I thought it was you who found me. But for eight months, I carried around such hateful anger. And then two weeks ago, I learned that you were shot. That you couldn't be there or come see me. And, I thought," she started do cry louder. "I thought you'd been killed. I was so crushed that I almost had a seizure. I realised then that I'd rather be dead myself than to live in a world I didn't belong in. I could never belong in a world if my very heart had died. You are my heart Wesley. You have my heart. And right now it's…" Kristen sucked in a quick breath, "…breaking."

The rattling sound of chains beneath the table made her gasp with fright.

The table vibrated as swarthy calloused tattooed hands slammed onto the table opposite her.

She was violently startled.

The breath left her lungs.

The series of flips and twists in her stomach brought on a fresh rush of nausea and her eyes seemed to focus on those hands.

His hands.

They were solidly cuffed, but they didn't belong to Wesley.

Green ink tattoos stained his hands like a magazine collage. His fingernails were long and black with grime. Many small scars were visible too. One between his thumb and his index finger looked like a crescent shaped row of incisions. It was a bite mark. A nasty, but healed stitched wound ran from the base of his middle finger of the other hand and disappeared under the sleeve of his dungaree.

Her vision suddenly grew cloudy, and then she remembered to breathe. Her gaze moved slowly from his scarred hands to his neck that was now visible.

A series of green tattoos were there too.

They didn't look anything close to the trendy tattoos that Freda, Dianna and Kristen herself sported. These were mean angry markings.

His cheeks were covered in a thick matted beard. His bottom lip sported a healing scar where it had been slit open. The hard straight mouth showed no hint of emotion.

The once perfect nose that he so fondly grazed over her cheek looked as though it had been broken, but not properly set. His thick lashes still swept the top of his cheeks. His eyebrows were covered with his greasy hair.

Kristen's heart nearly exploded.

She watched, as his lashes seemed to lift in slow motion.

Eight months were suddenly compressed into that second that his dark familiar eyes fluttered open and fixed on hers.

Those were Wesley's eyes all right. Though they stared at her from someone else's face, they were his eyes. They were bloodshot and flat.

He didn't blink.

He just stared at her.

For an undetermined amount of time all she could do was to stare back at him in complete and utter shock. Her entire body went numb in silent distress.

She watched as his gaze raked her face slowly, but without a flicker of interest or emotion. Tears streamed down her face, blurring her vision again. This time she gave in to a fit of crying. She wanted him to hold her the way he used to. She *needed* him to hold and promise her that things were going to be okay; that this was only a bad dream.

Somehow she felt that if she'd fall asleep at that moment, someone would wake her up and she'd be laying beside him in a tangle of sheets. But she knew that wasn't going to happen. She also knew that she wasn't entirely certain of the depth of this situation. Right at that moment his reaction had unnerved her completely.

Then like a blizzard over a millpond, his crackling voice froze her.

"I've made it clear to Clarke that I didn't want to see you."

Kristen pursed her lips to stop them from quivering.

His voice was low and monotonous, "You make me sick. I want you out of here."

"You don't mean that, Wesley," she croaked. "I know you don't mean that. You love me. I love you."

"You lied to me. You made me fall in love with a woman that didn't even exist. You made me fall in love with a ghost."

Kristen shook her head. "That's not true!"

"Oh but it is. Isn't your name Montello?"

His eyes burned hers. She nodded in defeat. "I was born a Montello, yes. But Wesley –"

He snorted in disgust, "Heiress to a narcotics empire and owner of the Krimson Kimono. Here I felt like an idiot! Why didn't you tell me?" he banged his bound hands on the small table. "WHY!"

In one smooth motion, he was on his feet and the table shot to the far side of the room. He towered over her then.

She rose shakily to her feet. "Wesley, please calm down."

"I WILL NOT CALM DOWN!!" He yelled at her. Rage was evident in his eyes. "Damn you Kristen Montello! Damn you!" He shrugged away from the hand she reached out to him.

"Please let me explain."

"No! I know all about your history! Your father paid me a visit before I got shot."

"I'm sorry..." Kristen couldn't get the right words out.

"You're sorry? I'm sorry, Kristen. I'm sorry I ever went to that stupid gay show. I'm sorry I ever laid eyes on you. My parents are dead because of *you*! I will never be able to work again because of *you*! I am in this hellhole BECAUSE OF YOU!"

"I know! And I'm sorry, Wesley!" she stumbled backwards against the solid wall. "But I had to run. I had to run away from my past. I had to leave my family behind – especially my father!" she had gotten him to listen. "I came to South Africa to start a new life. I had to make a living. I used all my savings – money I earned waiting tables and babysitting and working at the library over ten years. Pocket money and a trust fund my mother's family left me. That's the money that financed the Krimson Kimono. I hated my father! I hated my brother and I sure as hell hated being one of them!

"This was the last place on earth I thought my father would ever be looking for me. It was pure coincidence that he showed up here. I didn't know about his involvement in the local drug industry. Let alone that my brother was your boss!" She drew in a few shallow breaths. "You weren't supposed to happen to me Wesley. I wasn't supposed to fall in love. All I wanted was to be a part of the performing arts and a shot at being a success.

"But I don't regret loving you. And yes, I lied about my name. It's not Kristen Katts. It's Kristina Katherine Montello, daughter of Katerina Clara Putin and Lutzio Montello.

"My father was a poor fishmonger who met my Russian mother at the Campo de' Fiori market in Rome. She was there as a tourist. He married her for the fortune bequeathed to her as a sole survivor of her family. My money isn't blood money Wesley.

"I was ten when I found out that his businesses ran into the pits of hell. By the start of the next school year, I'd insisted on being schooled in England. I tried to run away from him before. But they kept finding me, Wesley. My brother dragged me kicking and screaming from Auckland in New Zealand two years ago. And the day of Jacques's murder, he had beaten me up so badly. I had to leave. But, the marks didn't just go away and you saw how severe it was." She expected more of a reaction from him, but he remained still.

He didn't move.

Nor did he blink.

He just fixed her with the same flat bottomless dark eyes.

"This is who I am. This is who I've always been. I'm asking you to forgive me for being Lutzio Montello's daughter."

They stood in silence and stared at one another.

His voice was yet again monotonous and unfeeling. "I can't forgive you."

Kristen flinched as though he'd struck her.

Her knees threatened to buckle under her, but she forced herself to move. She put one foot in front of the other as she kept her eyes focused on the ground ahead of her.

This was it.

She gave him one last look from over her shoulder. "I will never forgive myself," she said and closed the door behind her.

She stood against the closed door.

Three pairs of moist eyes stared back at her.

The last thing she saw was Kieran rushing to her before she passed out cold.

Darkness enveloped the confines of his cell that so resembled a birdcage. Wesley lay stretched out on the tiny twin bed. He couldn't think of anything but Kristen. The smell of her perfume had stayed on him. Every time he moved his head he could smell the floral scent of her. Her hair was cut like a pixie's. Little scars ran down the side of her ear. Rough dark patches on her skin made her look like a bruised peach.

He hated himself for becoming a monster.

He was a murderer, for God's sake!

He flexed his shoulders to release some of the tension in them, but was unsuccessful. He remembered the terrified look on her face when he'd opened his eyes.

She was afraid of him.

And, then her fear dissolved the next instant and she looked at him with such tenderness that almost made him cry.

But, he didn't cry.

He hadn't cried since he found out that she had lied to him.

He was angry with her.

He had hated her for what she'd done to him.

And then today she showed up in black skinny jeans, cowboy boots and a beige corduroy jacket over a leopard print shirt.

He cringed at the uncontrollable words that burned his tongue like venom. The truth was he did forgive Kristen when he'd gotten his wish.

When he'd thought that she'd died.

He made a pact with the devil himself.

He was ready to sell his soul so that she could live.

He was prepared to spend the rest of his days burning in hell just to have her back, even just for a day.

He wanted to hear her say that she loved him one last time.

And, today, that pact was fulfilled.

But, instead of allowing her to hold him the way he knew she wanted to – the way he'd wanted her to - he had pushed her away. He didn't hate her, despite what he'd said.

The truth was that he hated himself.

He hated what he'd become in prison.

He hated what he felt was necessary to do to survive.

He wasn't good enough for Kristen Katts.

He growled at himself.

Kristen Montello, he corrected. Kristen Katts was gone forever. She didn't even exist to begin with. So then what was he laying awake beating himself up for?

He knew the answer to that.

She'd told him that she'd dreamed of having a shot at success. And, he knew that that she'd never be successful with a convicted felon in her life. He had to let her go, and if lying was the way to go, then so be it. In a few days he would be a free man. He would have a different name and a fabricated past. He could live anywhere in the world and he had a pretty good idea where he'd choose.

# CHAPTER FIFTEEN

### *The Krimson Kimono, Greenpoint, Cape Town*
### *24 April 2009*

It was strange how quickly one could blend into society again and fall into old habits, Kristen thought as she leaned against the outside wall of the Krimson Kimono. She took a drag of the menthol cigarette as Natasha babbled on about the franchise Kristen was opening in Johannesburg.

"The crime rate is really bad there. I hope you know that. Melville is not what it used to be ten years ago."

Kristen flicked the ash from the tip of her cigarette. "I know what you're trying to do, Nat. I can't be here. I have to leave. It's just temporary, but at least there won't be any journalists bugging me, or the constant dread of running into..." her voice trailed off.

Natasha nodded. "Yes. You're right." She took a few lengthy drags of her fag before talking again. "You invited those two crazy girls over for your farewell?"

Kristen laughed. "Freda and Dianna are not as crazy as you make them out to be."

"I'm sure," Natasha raised a theatrical brow before flicking her bud into the night. "You're coming to give me a hand with those cases of beer?"

Kristen nodded. "I thought you were going to vote."

Natasha grimaced. "Not after Wicked Wilhelmina's daughter was arrested for the transporting of narcotics and driving under the influence of alcohol, I'm not."

Kristen shrugged as they went through the swing door into the kitchen. "I sure missed out on a heck of a lot."

"You sure did," Ling's voice sounded from the chest freezer. "It's weird now that we all know you're the boss. I always pictured Miss Montello to be a warrior princess with a whip and a kinky leather outfit."

The kitchen staff burst out laughing.

Kristen turned to Ling and giggled. "What makes you think that I don't have a whip and kinky clothes?"

The girl in the red kimono uniform angled her head. "Hmm... you got that," she snapped her fingers, "sharp prim and proper look about you."

Kristen laughed. It felt good to feel an emotion beside sadness and emptiness. She turned to Natasha. "I forgot your lighter on the counter. I'll be right back for the cases." She turned on her heel and walked back into the bar.

Two men were waiting for her there. "Cash bar tonight ma'am?"

Kristen smiled and nodded. "Yes. What will you be having?"

"Two beers and two tequila shots."

"Coming up," she rang up their order, reached under the counter for two shot glasses and the bottle of tequila. She slid the two long neck bottles over the counter to them. "Will that be all?"

They nodded and headed back to their table.

She turned to put the tequila back on the glass shelf when the sound of her name froze her.

"We've been looking all over for you!" Dianna smiled. She was buttonholed by her handsome fiancé. "You do remember Dylan?"

Kristen smiled at him as she came around the counter, "Of course. How are you?"

"I've got no complaints. How are you?" Dylan asked with genuine concern.

Kristen nodded. "I'm recovering." She burned to ask about Wesley. She knew that Dylan had represented him in court. They were friends. Dianna had told her earlier that week, when she'd asked her to be a bride's maid that Wesley was living with Alan.

It seemed that over the past eight months a lot had changed. Freda and Alan were dating. Though, Freda called him a walking vibrator with a wallet when she was with Kristen and Dianna. But, it was clear that the two were smitten. It was weird how life had played itself out. The irony was that she and Wesley would never have that kind of love again. At least she knew she wouldn't find it with anyone else.

"Kristen!" Freda shrieked as she fought past a group of young women who blocked her way to the bar. "Kris! Guess what?!"

Kristen shrugged her shoulders and laughed at her friend's excitement. "What is it?"

Freda threw her arms around her friend with Alan in tow.

Dianna's eyes got big, "Oh my God! Please tell me that Alan proposed."

Freda rolled her eyes heavenward. "No! Though that might be nice..." she turned to Dianna then to Kristen. "I got a supporting role in the second season of the local drama series *Prep School*!"

"That's great!" Dianna launched herself at Freda, "Mazeltov!"

"Mazeltov," Kristen and Dylan's voices sounded together.

Dianna turned to Kristen apologetically, "Oh Kris! I forgot that you have no idea what *Prep School* is. It's a local fourteen episode series that is played out against the backdrop of Gordon's Bay. It was a hit around September. It focused on a Jewish girl and a Muslim girl who share a hostel room at a boarding school there. It features some really hectic religious issues."

"That's wonderful, Freda!" Kristen said with even more excitement.

"I get to play a teenager!"

Alan and Dylan laughed.

"What's so funny?" The girls asked in unison.

"Freda acts like a teenager most of the time. This role is right up her alley," Dylan chuckled. "Isn't lying about your age just a universal culture among girls?"

Freda's eyebrows rose overdramatically. "What do you know about culture, anyway?" her voice was spirited as she jabbed him on the chest. "A tub of yogurt has more culture than all Capetonian men put together."

"Oh stop teasing," Natasha's voice carried over to them from the bar. "Kitty is leaving us tomorrow after the wedding, so let's get on with this party."

Kristen untied her apron and dropped it on the counter. "Thank you, Nats."

Natasha winked at her boss and turned her attention to the door. Beyond the crowd streaming into the pub, a young man stood smoking against a car. There was something creepy about him. Even in the darkness, she could feel that he was keeping an eye on everybody that came and went. She walked closer to the entrance where she patted her pockets and fished out a slim menthol cigarette. She smoked leisurely, not taking her gaze from the mysterious man across the street. There was something familiar about him, but Natasha couldn't really tell. And then, she noticed his hand running through his hair. Good heavens. It was Wesley. "Wesley?" she called and started crossing the road. Natasha took a startled step back when she saw the deep scars on his clean-shaven face. "What in God's name did they do to you in there?" she reached out and cupped his face.

"They turned me into a beast. That's for sure." His voice was just the way she remembered it, except the hardened set of his face.

"What are you doing here? Why don't you come in? Kristen is inside. Should I call her out?"

He shook his head briskly. "No. I don't want to see her."

Natasha crossed one arm over her chest and puffed on her cigarette. "You mean, you don't want her to see you?" she searched his face. Something stirred in his eyes.

She sighed. "She loves you, you know. Now more than she ever did before. She doesn't talk about anything except business. That tells me that she is trying to deal with the void you left in her."

"Void?"

"She is just the shell of the person she was a year ago. I'd say you were the reason she always had a smile. These days she tries really hard to smile and laugh. Sometimes the effort is an altogether pathetic flop."

"You shouldn't call me by that name anymore," he flicked the butt of his filter cigarette into the wind. "It's going to rain tonight. I should go."

"Don't run Wesley. You will always be right there where you find yourself. You are the only person you cannot run from." Natasha took the last drag before stepping over the little burning ember with her sneaker. "She's leaving tomorrow night after the wedding. I'm sure you might have heard." With that she went back across the road and into the lively sports bar across from him.

Wesley slammed his fists against the car behind him. It was the first word he'd heard about it. Not Alan, Dylan or their girlfriends had mentioned it to him. Maybe it was his own fault. He did make it clear that he didn't want any update on Kristen Montello, after all. Yet, here he was standing across the street from her hip little establishment to make sure that her life continued as normal as possible, as he had done since his release. Tonight would be no different from the other nights. He would drive behind her at a safe distance and park in Queen Victoria Road and watch the lights go on in her apartment across the road in Wale Street. He'd sit there in the darkness and watch her bedroom window for hours after the lights had gone out.

The light drizzle had turned into a steady downpour.

Wesley wasn't sure how long he'd been standing in the rain. He was drenched from his long black pea coat, right through to his gray T-shirt and his dark blue denims. He'd had a haircut that was now fast becoming his old careless curls. The scars on his body, especially in his face, along with the aggressive tattoos won him cautious stares from strangers. Despite the neat, decent clothes he'd worn, the stigma attached to those horrid green markings on his flesh defied every physical scrap of decency in his immediate and indirect social groups. He felt inferior and embarrassed instead of the proud son-of-a-bitch his fellow inmates had gotten to know.

He'd been watching the entrance of the Krimson Kimono, but only just realised that he'd dwelled too much on fantasies that he hadn't even realised that Dylan and Alan were steering their dates toward their cars. Right on cue, Kristen was at the door waiting for the last of her staff to leave. The flashing red light above the door was in the shape of a kimono. It went out the minute the door was locked.

Wesley got behind the wheel of his car.

Freda's voice had grabbed his attention. He couldn't make out what she was saying, but she was making hand gestures to Kristen who was now unlocking the driver's side of her shiny silver Peugeot 206. He would have thought that she'd splashed out and gotten the top of the range car, but she'd remained true to herself.

He wanted her to fail.

He wanted her to stumble into the path of wickedness so that he had a reason to hate her. He was obsessed with finding a flaw. The truth was, he realised to his dismay, that Kristen had no flaws. The only flaw she had was him.

He followed her car to a familiar location in Bothasig, Milnerton. It was a short drive out of the city. The house belonged to Dylan and Dianna. Wesley slowed down and carried on straight past the turnoff. It helped that Dylan had chosen a corner plot. The location of the house was such that Wesley could view it from three different angles. A little recreational park was beside Dylan's opposite neighbour. The park could be accessed from either side of the crescent and that's where Wesley decided to park in his stakeout.

The storm had hit without warning.

Kristen hated driving in the rain. She'd known it was a stupid idea to drive all the way from Greenpoint to Bothasig to go for a final fitting at 3am. She looked on the clock on the dashboard. It was nearly 4am. At the speed she was driving, she'd be lucky if she got home before 04:30am.

The road works at the Paarden Eiland turnoff was full of potholes and gravel. The rain beating down on her windshield made it near impossible to see. It wasn't as though she could just pull off the road.

There was a car trailing her. The driver seemed to be quite content at her tail since she'd signaled the car to pass her a couple of kilometers down the N1.

She was freezing. All she wanted was to feel hot water over her entire body. She could barely feel her toes. At least she didn't have to walk in the rain after she parked her car in the basement of her apartment block.

Adderley Street was blissfully empty. It seemed that she'd lost her tail at the foreshore. She drove with added confidence as she rounded the bend at the Company Gardens. In no time she was safely parked. She fished her keys out of her bag and jogged over to the stairs that led into the brightly lit ground floor. Sipho was ready to greet her with a smile. She must have looked as cold and tired as she felt. He set her safely in the lift and gave her a fond salute.

Kristen almost gave in to the reverie of her flopping onto her bed and pulling the thick warm quilt over her head and sleeping until Freda called her awake at 10am.

The doors slid open in their liquid fashion. Kristen slouched toward her apartment. Once she locked the door, she flung her bag to the floor and started undressing as she made her way to her bedroom. She was naked by the time she strode through the dark room. With the light of the en suite flicked on the bedroom seemed even more inviting.

Water shot out of the large showerhead. And, true to deep sorrow, she cried under the comfort of the gushing water for the one man she feared she'd never hold again.

*She was crying.*

Wesley could hear her from the bathroom across the hall. He'd used the extra key she'd given him last year to let himself in. He knew he'd beat her to her apartment if he'd taken an alternate route. And, after three minutes of waiting, he'd heard her key in the lock. He watched her from beside the sofa where he'd crouched into a ball.

He wasn't expecting a strip show, but Kristen had given him the full monty. She made quick work of the long black dress, her coat and her heels. Her stockings and her underwear made for a drooling silent encore. She was beautiful. Even with the silvery pink scars on her upper back and high up on one of her thighs. He wanted to throw himself at her feet, but he didn't dare at the risk of scaring her. Once he heard the shower doors closed, he stripped out of his wet clothes and scooped it up along with hers. He dumped the clothes in the laundry basket in the main bathroom before turning on the smaller shower in there for the water to heat.

Silently, and carefully, he moved back into her bedroom and opened the cupboard she'd once reserved for him. His clothes were just as he'd left them. It was terribly outdated by now, but the crisp feel of clean clothes felt wonderful under his touch. He pulled out a pair of black sweats from a pile and a dark jumper from another rack. His socks and white mini briefs were still on the bottom shelf, along with cologne and deodorant.

It was as though nothing had changed. His eye fell on the dressing table where he witnessed his hairbrush beside hers.

Had Kristen really been living with the ghost of him? He was grief-stricken at the thought. He shuffled back into the bathroom across the hall where he welcomed the hot water over his aching body. Once he'd dried himself and dressed, he checked his reflection in the mirror. He was still just a shadow of his old self. It was right then that he heard the sound that had caused him near insanity less than a year ago.

Kristen was crying. It was gut-wrenching to listen to her sob. The ache in her voice crippled him when she cried out his name repeatedly on the other side of the wall.

How in the name of all that was good could she cry like that over him? He needed to get out of there, before she saw him. He'd wanted to make sure that she was all right, and now that he knew that she was, he had to leave.

"I'm a fool," Kristen said to the empty room once she'd slipped into her oversized tunic and shorts. She towel-dried her hair and walked over to her dressing table. She pulled a comb through her hair carefully, not to disturb the tender stitches on the crown of her head. Her puffy red eyes made her look ten years older. She shrugged at the task that lay ahead before she faced her cold empty bed alone.

Her clothes she'd shed on her way in.

She moaned in protest, but forced herself off the bed. Wesley had always been firm about dirty laundry.

Kristen bent over at the door and reached to the floor at the place where her panties should have been. She staggered a bit before straightening.

Despite the fact that she was exhausted, she still had her wits about her. She took a step into the passageway. Her eyes stayed glued to the floor. There were no clothes in sight.

Kristen was suddenly wide-awake. Her sixth sense kicked in.

A woman's instinct was always spot on. She willed herself to remain calm. Beside the missing clothes, everything else seemed normal. If someone was in her apartment, she had to call the police.

The only problem was that her bag was next to the door where she'd dropped it when she came in. The telephone was in the kitchen.

She was stuffed, a sitting duck.

Then, as she drew in a shaky breath, she saw the wet track marks on the bathroom tiles opposite her bedroom. It was a large print. It was slightly smudged as though someone had tried to wipe it.

Her heart slammed against her chest in a painfully exhausting gallop. She was breaking out in a cold sweat. She reached behind the bedroom door and unhooked one of her electric guitars. She held it like a baseball bat – ready to swing.

To hell with the downstairs security, Kristen thought. Anyone off the street could get into the building. Management was sure going to get an earful from her, that was, Kristen thought nervously, if she survived to tell the tale.

She took a deep breath. Then, with courage of a Herculean, she stormed into the bathroom with growing rage expanding every cell in her body, and giving an unconsecrated scream. Whoever was in the bathroom would be behind the door and come hell or high water, she was going to draw blood from the bastard. As true as Bob, she'd heard the strangled moan when she struck. It was a male cry she heard. And, as she expected, he was wrestling the instrument come weapon from her with less than forced effort.

He'd twisted her arm slightly in a stinging maneuver that sent the guitar sliding across the bathroom.

She was slapping and clawing all the while she screamed. A heavy calloused hand slapped her mouth shut, and she tried kicking but he sidestepped and stumbled, taking her with him to the ground.

"Kristen! It's okay! It's all right. It's me! It's Wesley."

She was delusional! Was she just imagining it? Very cell in her body went numb. Her raspy throat made her eyes tear. Above all else, the familiar scent of him drowned her senses and her eyes fluttered open.

"I'm going to take my hand away from your mouth, but you have to promise me that you will not scream." His voice was low, yet not as gentle as she remembered.

"Good girl," he said when she remained silent. "Did you hurt your head?" he was crouched beside her now as he helped her into a sitting position, while examining her face in his hands.

"Wesley?" she choked out, wondering if she'd imagined it. "Wesley?"

He stilled her face with his hands. Her eyes seemed disbelieving. "Yes, Kitten. It is me." He pressed his lips to her temple. Her damp hair smelled like a fresh burst of herbal fusion.

"You scared me."

"I'm sorry. I wanted to leave, but then you came out of the shower too fast. I didn't want to scare you. I would have left the moment I could without being noticed."

She touched a hand to his cheek. "Why? Why didn't you want to see me?"

"I wanted to see you. I wanted to make sure that you're okay."

Her arms stole around his neck, her heart in her throat. "Does that mean you've forgiven me?"

Wesley didn't hide that he was crying, because there were tears in Kristen's eyes too. "Oh Kristen… I've cursed you so much. I've hated you so much, but when you walked out of that visiting room, I was the one who was condemned. No amount of time in hell could compare to what I felt at that moment.

"When I said I could never forgive you, I wasn't talking about you, Kitty. I was talking about me."

"Does this mean… that you still love me? Does this mean that you want me back? What does this mean for us?"

There was intensity in her eyes that made his chest swell painfully. "I love you, Kristen, but… I can't… We can't… Not after…" A frustrated growl ripped from his throat as he jumped to his feet, his hands locked behind his head.

Kristen struggled to her feet clumsily. Her entire being trembled. Her knees turned to jelly. His incomplete attempts at justifying – justifying what exactly? She shook her head unable to comprehend the obvious conclusion he'd drawn for her. Nothing could be clearer. A fresh rush of tears filled her eyes. "This is me on my knees Wesley. I'm begging you to love me enough."

He looked up and met her gaze steadily, wiping his tears with the heels of his palms. "Kristen you deserve better –"

"No Goddammit!" She yelled. "You either love me the way I love you or you don't! You either want me Wesley, or you don't! Because God knows I want *you* – all of *you*!"

He was on his feet in an instant. The move was so fast, Kristen's head reeled. His mouth claimed hers in an assault so passionate, that she held onto his arms for support.

His kisses were stripping her of her sense of self as they always had. And, without warning he lifted her off the ground and carried her into the bedroom. The shadows cast by the light from the en suit set the room in a strangely maudlin atmosphere, yet melancholy was threaded heavily like a tapestry of contrast in a needlepoint masterpiece.

It had been eight months since they had made love. Her skin was as soft as it was the first time he'd touched her. Her mouth was still as sweet, and her hair… Oh lord, her hair didn't fall over her face in unruly curls as it did before. Her thick locks wouldn't sweep over his naked chest the way he remembered. It was a huge reminder of what she survived. The short pixie style added a good few years to her face. It still had the same cashmere feel to it.

If it was possible, he loved her right at that moment more than he had ever loved her before. More than he ever could love anyone in a million lifetimes.

He hadn't expected her to, but she opened her eyes while kissing him back. He was lost in those deep green pools that drew him into her soul.

"Wesley... There is something I have to tell you."

"It can wait," he breathed against her mouth. He kissed her again and again. His hands trailed down her body until he found the folds of her womanhood. She was slick and ready, just as ready as he was for her. He slid into her with slow, careful thrusts. His heart threatened to seize in the delightful pleasure he felt when they'd become one being.

Her tongue flickered and probed, he granted her access to the warmth of his mouth.

Wesley was all man, inside and out. He made love to her painfully slow, so gentle that when she opened her eyes she found him staring down at her with such ardor; it sent her heart beating faster. His mouth lowered to her neck. He kissed every tiny welt that was proof of the scalding fire she'd survived. It felt as though he was trying to kiss them away as a parent magically kissed away the pains of a toddler. And then she felt it. The intensity of her desire as Wesley drove her to her peak. It came crashing over her like an avalanche, sending her body in a series of rapid contractions that swept him over the brink of sanity along with her. They held on to each other. Somehow Kristen knew that nothing would ever be the same from here on out. She knew it because beyond his emotional smile, he had *goodbye* written all over his face.

# CHAPTER SIXTEEN

*Wale Street, CBD, Cape Town*
*25 April 2009*

Kristen woke without stirring.

She opened her eyes to find that Wesley was lying on his back beside her. Last night had been unfathomable. She listened to the peaceful breaths he took. His sleep relaxed face was stripped of the tension she'd seen last night.

She got a glimpse of the scars on his face. Now that his face was free of the matted beard, she saw the deep crater-like wound beneath his cheekbone. A series of untidy stitches ran from the middle of his forehead through a tiny gap in his eyebrows and ended a few millimeters under one sooty brow. The bridge of his nose was unnaturally lumpy and the cut she'd seen on his lip the day at the prison left a tiny white slash in his lip line.

She felt his hands roaming over her body as he studied each new scar with his rough, calloused hands. He'd become more buff since the last time she'd seen him. The green tattoos were completely exposed now, yet somehow they seemed to be faded somewhat. There was, however, one on his arm that made her teary again. It was the silhouette of a black cat. Not just any cat, but a kitten. Symbolic maybe? She was too afraid to hope.

"That one's real."

His voice startled her. She sunk deeper into the bed, eyes wide.

"The rest are only temporary. Clarke thought it would be advantageous to sport some tacky *tjapies*." He smiled at her lazily. "*Tjapies* is Cape Flats slang for *tattoos*."

Kristen went into his arms at the gesture he made with his arm, "I believe so."

He toyed with her hair, massaging the uneven row of stitches on her scalp.

"They had to shave my hair off. It was badly scourged from the fire. And the lump you're feeling is where I hit my head against the curb when I fell out of the car."

He buried his face in her hair, breathing in its fresh, clean scent. There were so many things he wanted to say, but he held her to him instead.

The telephone rang from the kitchen making Kristen groan, "And so starts the first day of the rest of my life." She propped up on one arm, dropping a kiss on his mouth. "You want some coffee?"

"Yes. Please." He watched her pull her tunic over her head as she went out the bedroom door reluctantly, only pausing to pick up the guitar that lay near the entrance of the main bathroom. He heard her muffled voice as she answered the phone.

Wesley shrugged out of bed. He took a peek out the window. Rain clouds gathered low over the mountain, a gray mist heavy over the part of town visible from the window. He walked over to the dressing table, sneezing suddenly. Since everything seemed unchanged, he pulled open the top drawer where Kristen kept a box of pop-up facial tissues. He was spot on. It sat right at the front of the drawer beside a familiar item he'd parted with the night of the explosion. It was the ring he'd hoped eight months ago that Kristen would accept as a token of their love. The night he'd wanted to propose.

Freda had called two hours earlier than they'd agreed at the fitting. Kristen glanced at the clock in the kitchen as she poured two cups of coffee and placed a jar of rusks on the table. She moved the guitar slightly back and out of the danger of an accidental coffee spill. Turning at the smell of his cologne, she found him leaning against the entryway to the kitchen. They stood there, staring at each other for a solid minute, before the silence became too loud.

Wesley took a seat opposite her at the counter. He only wore a pair of faded blue jeans and a brown towel around his defined shoulders. His damp hair was combed back. Finger tracks left it looking as careless and sexy as ever.

Somehow, she felt as though she was treading on eggshells. His voice sounded low and nonchalant when he spoke. "It's going to be a cold and wet one. It's quite a change from last year, don't you think?"

Kristen frowned in confusion.

"The weather," he raised his brows, taking a sip of his coffee, in answer to her unspoken question.

*The weather.* How very insignificant compared to a few hours ago when he'd shown her how much pleasure his love for her had brought to both of them.

He reached into his pocket and pulled out a cigarette and a lighter. He lit the tip and inhaled deeply, scanning her face. She looked every bit as tense as he felt. Upon exhaling he leaned forward slightly, "Have you been playing at all?"

Kristen pulled the guitar from the counter, into her lap. She shook her head. "No. Between the Krimson Kimono and art exhibitions I didn't have much time."

He listened to the clumsy fingers tugging at the strings. "Art exhibitions?" he didn't miss the nervous flicker in her eyes.

"Yes I've met a local artist whose work is inspired by the baroque era. The canvases all hold the most beautiful fountains in Rome, and others of tourist attractions."

"You could sound a little more enthusiastic," he mocked, smiling. "You know how baroque allows me to focus."

"I remember," she gave the tiniest smile.

He drained his mug and concentrated on the remainder of his cigarette. "What's wrong, Kitty Cat?"

Kristen dropped the instrument to the ground with a thump. She risked a sweeping look at him from under her lashes, "Am I going to see you again?"

Wesley should have known better than to come here last night. Kristen wasn't the kind of woman who skimmed the surface of a situation. And, how could he forget that she was the one person that knew him almost better than he knew himself. He killed his cigarette in the empty mug, fixing a steady gaze on her. "No. I go into protective custody from today on. I'm moving up country."

Kristen almost yelled out at him. He'd hurt her again, "And what of us? What about last night?"

Wesley swallowed the lump in his throat. The look on Kristen's face was anticipation... for the worst news. "Weren't we comforting each other last night?" he asked. "There is nothing more to it, is there?"

Kristen would never be able to explain where her courage and control had come from when she spoke through the pain. He was tearing her apart with deliberate slowness. His thoughtless words sliced through her heart with the same preciseness as a samurai sword did a cashmere scarf.

The truth knocked the very breath out of her.

She licked her suddenly dry lips. She was too weak to protest. She knew she would never survive more of his insensitive yakking. She also knew that no matter how much she loved Wesley Johnson, she also loved Kristen Montello, and Wesley Johnson was oblivious to the fact that he was killing her with his foolish mind games.

Her eyes felt strangely dry and stingy, but she just could not cry, "You may be right about a lot of things Wesley. But last night had nothing to do with comfort." She had surprised him; she could see it as his eyes narrowed, "At least not for me." The absence of emotion in his eyes nearly toppled her off the chair.

Kristen rose to her feet. "I have to get going. I have a wedding to live through." She gave him a long assessing look before she managed a very tiny smile. "You are welcome to stay as long as you need to. I won't be back here for a while." She shuffled back to the bedroom, and into the shower.

When she returned fully dressed, keys and duffle bag in hand, the apartment was spotless. She stood rooted in the lounge. She could smell his cologne, as though he'd just stepped out to get the newspaper around the corner in St George's Mall. But, she knew better. She knew that Wesley was gone, and she was alone in the apartment.

She walked over to the sliding door that led out to her balcony. While rain and wind rattled the glass, she pulled the blinds open, leaned her head against the cool glass. That's when she saw him standing on the traffic island in the middle of Wale Street, between wild-branched palm trees. The daunting black sky seemed to descend to the slopes of Cape Town's steep roads.

His black coat was draped over a shoulder. His arms were stretched out sideways, his face turned up to the sky. The picture was so typical Wesley. He loved this kind of weather. He'd once told her that he believed as a child that rain was the blessings God bestowed on parched souls.

Kristen allowed herself to really look at the crazy man in the rain. He was free. But was that freedom really worth living without the kind of beauty they shared last night? He sure fooled her in thinking so. So it was the perfect man was just a naïve daydream she'd lived with for a year. She sadly mistook the Wesley of last night for someone who gave a damn – someone like herself. She'd held her bruised heart out for him to mend, but this morning he'd trampled all over it. Kristen pulled away from the window, and with a last look around, she pulled the door closed behind her.

Wesley welcomed the downpour of rain. It wasn't as before when he needed that little faith and the rain seemed to clear his mind so that he could think straight. Kristen hadn't said a word about his puckered gunshot wounds, his scars from his stay in prison. She was clearly in denial; pretending things were as it were before. Then, he remembered the wedding. Dylan had told him that the ceremony would take place in the St Mary's Anglican Church in Stellenbosch. He hadn't asked Wesley to be his best man, nor to be a groom's man. The green-eyed monster stirred inside of him. Alan and Freda had discussed the bride's maids' dresses so many times over the past few weeks. He knew it was burnt orange in colour and a very straightforward pattern that Kristen had chosen. Wesley knew from experience that Kristen had a unique eye for elegance and style. The thought that another man would escort her into a church in that bride's maid dress had him sprinting to the green Ford Escort that he'd acquired over the past month. Even if he had to watch from a distance, he needed to know who was touching her. How he'd survive when she moved up to Johannesburg was beyond imagining. He pretended that the fierce thudding of his heart was just his concern for the wet road ahead, and the moist on his eyelashes – the sting of the wind.

He took the Sable Road turnoff on the N1 and headed for Canal Walk. There was no way he could show up at Dylan's wedding in soaked denims and a pea coat.

Wesley skimmed the shops until he found a suit outlet. A flash of colour in his peripheral vision drew his attention. He turned in the direction of the hair and nail salon on the lower deck. As fate would have it, Kristen and Dianna stood blowing on their fresh manicures while Freda ranted on and on about the hairdresser who was late. He heard Dianna's voice clearly, "At least our nails and makeup are all done." He stood out of their view, in the entrance of the suit outlet. Freda came into view. "At least we'll all be dressed by twelve. Couldn't we just do our own hair, Annie?"

Kristen looked weary. Had he been the cause of that look? He heard her voice so clearly, it sounded like whisper carried on the wind. "That is the best idea you've come up with in the past two weeks."

Freda pulled a face that made Dianna laugh. "Easy for you to say," Freda buttonholed both girls as they started for an exit. "You're lucky not to have share in our hair emergencies."

Wesley watched them until they were out of sight. He checked the time on his wrist. There were two hours left before the ceremony was due to start. The vibration in his pocket broke his concentration. It was Alan calling. "Yes Alan."

"Man, are you all right? You didn't call last night and I thought that something had happened to you."

"I'm good Alan. I'm just at the mall."

"The mall?" Alan yawned. "Well, Dylan and I are at the flat. The girls are going to be at Dylan's. We wish you'd reconsider going with us."

"I might show up."

"Wesley," Alan's voice sounded strained. "You *must* go."

"Ja... I'll make an appearance at the church." He heard a rustle on the other end. Dylan's voice beamed through the earphone, "An appearance? That's bullshit man! I'm tired of your sulking, Wesley! It's time that you get a grip on yourself. We all want you there. We need you there."

Wesley bit back the urge to confront his friend. There could only be one reason why Dylan had not asked him to be a part of his wedding entourage, and that was because he was embarrassed by Wesley. "Very well. I'll meet you at the church."

The drive to the Cape Winelands took longer than he'd expected. He had to take a detour through Eerste River and over the N2 bridge that led him to the Polkadraai Road, and back on to the Stellenbosch Arterial. The short drive into the town seemed to go on forever. And then, the front of his car seemed to drop. It became impossible to steer and he eased it off the road with instinct. A flat tyre was a son-of-a-bitch. By the time he'd changed the wheel and pulled the black and white pinstripe jacket of his designer suit back over his white woolen polo neck, the wedding had surely started. At this rate, he might miss the ceremony altogether. Then again, Dylan was his best friend, and had always only been good to him. So, he swallowed his pride, and started up the car again.

The parking area at the church was packed. Wesley saw the white wedding limousine. The door was opened slightly.

And, true to Freda's description, the burnt orange dress she wore was truly exquisite. She either didn't see him, or she hadn't recognised him with his dark glasses. The priest appeared in the door where he motioned to Freda. His black robe and white collar seemed ill fitting for the occasion.

Wesley strained to hear the priest, his eyes focused on the doorway behind him for a glimpse of the other bride's maid, but he could not see Kristen close to Freda. He turned to find that the bride was backing out of the car. Through the long white layers of her veil, he could see the Austrian crystals worked all over the gown. It was a bride's fairytale gown if ever he saw one. The Chinese-like design at the top and the long sweeping elegance of the slightly flared dress was a little on the modest side for a bride like Dianna, but the bridal satin and charming lace hugged her figure tastefully. A traditional, Christian bride - there was nothing more beautiful.

Wesley turned to find both the bride's maids in the archway that led to the entrance of the church. *Here Comes the Bride*, wedding march sounded through the windows of the small church. And, then he took a closer look to see her. But, Kristen wasn't one of the bride's maids standing in wait on the stone steps of the church.

Wesley did a double take. His heart sank.

Dianna and Freda wore more than identical dresses and hairstyles. They also held twin expressions of doubt, though they smiled supportively at the bride who was already starting to them slowly. He could still only see the back of her and when she came to a halt at the bottom step, she turned her face up to the two bride's maids.

It all happened so quickly; Wesley struggled to find his voice. He was suffocating by the scene that played out before him. If Dianna and Freda were bride's maids then – the bride turned around in that heart-stopping moment that sent him storming forward – Kristen was the blushing bride.

Wesley tried shaking the image from his head.

Maybe it was posttraumatic stress that was making him hallucinate. But no matter how hard he shook his head, Kristen's face remained.

He heard the airy gasps from the top of the stairs. He wasn't sure what Freda had said, but out of the corner of his eye, he saw Dianna clasp her hands over her tiny bouquet, shrieking with glee.

There were tons of lead in his knees that made walking impossible, but he willed himself to walk up to her.

His hands stole around her arms as he gave her a light shake, "What the hell is going on, Kitten?" He searched her wide green eyes that were filled with a jumble of emotions.

Kristen shook her head in protest. "Wesley…" she breathed. "What are you doing here?"

"Why are you wearing this dress? I don't understand." His jaw was tightly spun as it throbbed violently. "What is all this Kristen?"

"The first day of the rest of my life," she dropped her gaze for a second. When she met his eyes again, he'd become a blur.

Wesley's eyes bore into hers. Reality hit him right in the chest with the same impact of the bullet that had almost cost him his life in June of last year. That's what she'd said to him this morning before she rushed to answer the telephone.

*And so starts the first day of the rest of my life. I have a wedding to live through.*

"No," Wesley shook his head. "No. You would never do this to me. You would never let another man touch you."

Kristen shrugged out of his grasp. "You have no claim over me, Wesley Johnson!" A burst of rage and anger exploded within her. She smacked him repeatedly with the bouquet of yellow and orange roses against his chest in a crisscross motion that sent the delicate heads of the flowers and its petals floundering to the ground like confetti. "You are the one who told me that there was nothing more to last night!"

The commotion behind him, made them both turn in mutual bewilderment. Dylan an Alan stood on either side of a slight man Wesley remembered being introduced to at some point in the past. He was the artist she had spoken about that morning. His name was Benedict Forlani. He noticed all at once that his two friends were trying to hold back the fuming groom. The congregation had scattered all around the bridal entourage to see what the commotion was all about. Freda's encouraging, but quivering smile complimented Dianna's hopeful nod.

Kristen shook her head in mortification.

How loud had she been talking? What had they heard?

She scooped up the skirts of her dress and started running across the luscious green courtyard that led to the ample gardens of the wine farm the church was built on.

Wesley started after her. He was a good twenty feet behind her but he managed to meet up with her. "Kristen!"

"Go away!" she shouted over her shoulder at him. She had no idea when and how her shoes had slipped out of her feet, but at that point she was shoeless. She kept running through the wet grass. "Leave me alone!" She wasn't even sure that she knew where she was going. All she knew was that she had to get away from Wesley.

He looked over his shoulder. They were just over a hundred feet away from the church, and they were still going. "Kristen!" He pushed himself harder and grasped her flailing arm, as the other held her dress. He spun her around, but the abrupt movement sent her slamming into his chest, and sent them both hitting the ground rolling over and over together until they came to a stop. Wesley was lying on top of her, both of them fighting for their breath.

He looked down at her pale face. Her eyes filled with stubborn tears. Too much time had passed.

No more mistakes. Wesley pressed his mouth against hers. The kiss was hard and ungentle. He coaxed her lips apart with his probing tongue.

Kristen hesitated, but then when she felt him slow down and stroke her face with such tenderness, she gave in to the petal soft kisses that he bestowed on her now.

He pulled one of her dainty hands in his, bringing it closer to his mouth. "Oh, Kitten..." he sighed against her fingertips as he kissed the palm side of her hands. "When I thought I'd lost you back there, I almost died. Never ever do that to me again. You are mine, Kristen. Mine alone."

She was laying flat on her back; Wesley pressed his forehead against hers, without their noses touching. "The night I thought you died in the explosion," he reached into his pocket and pulled out the ring she'd kept safe in her dressing table drawer. "I was going to ask you to marry me. I had it all worked out: rose petals in the bath, scented cinnamon candles, champagne, cherries and truffles. I planned to spend my life showing you how much I loved you."

Kristen let out a cry. This time it was a cry of joy. "But this morning... this morning you said –"

"I was stupid! I wasn't thinking, Kristen. What I said this morning… I wanted you to walk away without looking back. I wanted you to find what you came to this country for. I wanted you to have your shot at success."

"Don't you get it Wesley?" she searched his eyes, marveling at the way his tears made his lashes stick together.

He shook his head before opening his eyes. "No."

"Success means nothing to me if we're not working toward it together. I could never be complete without you."

"But Benedict…"

"Citizenship," that single word explained a heck of a lot. The faint drizzle around them turned into a light shower.

"Why not marry me instead?" he slipped the ring that had belonged to his mother, on her cold ring finger. "That's if forever isn't too much to ask."

Kristen met his lips with hers. She lifted her face to the sky as he had done earlier that morning. "Yes," she said. "Yes, I will marry you."

"All of me?" he teased.

"I'm happy with that."

Freda's voice sounded behind them, making them suddenly aware that they were not alone anymore, "See how the rain brings a clear mind?"

Wesley and Kristen turned in unison to find the limousine with Freda, Dianna and their partners streaming out of the car with the priest in tow. He shook his balding head in wonder, bible under his arm. "The Lord works in mysterious ways, doesn't he?"

Freda nudged the clergyman in the back with her usual over enthusiastic spirit. "Get on with it," she glanced around at everyone before adding less spirited as before, "In the name of God." She hurriedly made the sign of the cross.

Dianna bowed her head to hide her amusement. Biting down on her lips didn't help, because Wesley had thrown his head back and laughed.

Kristen took a panoramic view of her and Wesley's friends before locking gazes with him.

It seemed he was right about the rain on all levels. She grabbed hold of his hands and allowed him to pull her up onto her feet.

They'd paired up as though it was predestined, Kristen thought, joy flowing through her. From there on out she knew that everything was the way it was intended to be. Wesley was everything to her. And, at her side, he was in his right place.

--THE END--

# AFRIKAANS AND SOUTH AFRICAN SLANG REFERENCES USED IN THIS BOOK

*Suiping* is the Afrikaans slang word for *drinking* (usually alcohol)

*Boerseun* is an Afrikaans term describing a South African boy or young man of white Afrikaaner descent

*Broer* is the Afrikaans word for *brother*

*Ja* is the Afrikaans word for *yes*

*Boet* is the Afrikaans word for *brother*

*Blaartjies* is Afrikaans for *the* diminutive form of *leaves*. In this case it is associated with fruit tobacco which is popular in Cape Town, especially among students.

*Dagga* is South African slang word for *marijuana* or *cannabis*.

*Lekker* is the Afrikaans word for *nice*.

*En* is the Afrikaans word for *and*.

*'n* is the Afrikaans word for *a*.

*Ontbyt* is the Afrikaans word for *breakfast*.

*Botter* is the Afrikaans word for *butter*.

*Konfyt* is the Afrikaans word for *jam*.

*Respek* is the Afrikaans word for *respect*.

*Kaapse Klopse* is a minstrel festival that takes place annually on 2 January and it is also referred to as the *Coon Carnival* in Cape Town, South Africa

*"Daai sal alles wees vir nou, outjie"* is Afrikaans for *"That will be all for now, guy."*

*Nil per mond* is Afrikaans for a medical instruction meaning *"Nothing by mouth"*

Hoe lyk dit? Is Afrikaans for "how about it" in a suggestive context, although the direct English translation is "How does it look?"

*Tikkop* – is Afrikaans Cape Flats slang for a *crystal meth user*

*Tik lollie* is Afrikaans for a pipe-like device used to smoke crystal meth

*Hola* – is slang for "what's up" in South Africa, usually heard in Johannesburg

*Sorella* – Italian for *sister*

*Verkrampte* - conservative or reactionary, especially as regards apartheid

Boerewors – a traditional South African beef sausage

*Bergie* – Afrikaans Cape Flats slang for vagrant

*braaied wors* – Afrikaans for *barbequed or grilled sausage maar tog* – Afrikaans for *but still/ anyway*

*Ja baas* is Afrikaans for *yes boss*

*manskappe* is Afrikaans Cape Flats slang for *friends/ gang members*

*Pozzie* is South African slang for a *residence* in the context of one's physical home

*Dop* is Afrikaans Cape Flats slang for an *alcoholic beverage*

*Tjapies* is Afrikaans Cape Flats slang for *tattoos.*

# ABOUT THE AUTHOR

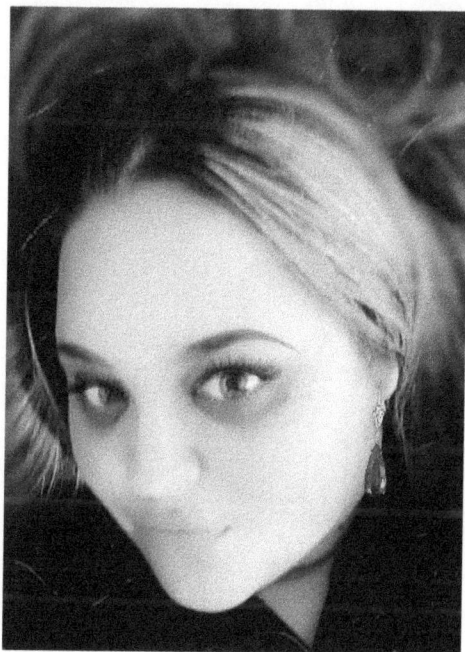

Olivia Parker is a South African-born writer. She studied journalism at the Cape Peninsula University of Technology and cut her professional teeth at The Star newspaper in Johannesburg as an entertainment journalist. Olivia has worked in various communication mediums as a journalist, radio talk show producer and media liaison among others. Olivia's keen interest in people, the arts and international relations has resulted in a lifetime's worth of poetry and manuscripts. Olivia currently resides in New Zealand and a part from writing, enjoys cooking and baking for her husband Wayne and three sons Reed, Wayrinley and Hayden.

CPSIA information can be obtained
at www.ICGtesting.com
Printed in the USA
LVHW010848160820
663317LV00002B/276